And Do Remember Me

MARITA GOLDEN

Ballantine Books • New York

146614399

FOR JOE, THE ONE
I WAITED FOR.

I wish to thank Dr. Endesha Ida Mae Holland, Dorie Ladner, Alberta Barnett and Lawrence Guyot for their time and assistance.

For B., I understand now.

And Do Remember Me

FREEDOM
SUMMER

J ESSIE FOSTER stood on the side of Highway 82, just outside Columbus, the Mississippi sun blistering her neck, tiny rivulets of perspiration huddled in her armpits. The once crisp wad of bills she had pinned to her brassiere, thirty-two dollars in fives and ones, lay wilted and damp against her skin. The white blouse she'd ironed that morning several hours before she took flight was covered by a thin film of dark Delta soil. Dry, breathless winds occasionally lifted the hem of her skirt and parched the skin of her thighs. The tissue with which she wiped her forehead was so moist from use that it crumbled in her hands, leaving tiny white specks scattered across her face. All the work she'd done on her hair before leaving and still she could feel it napping up at the edges, the roots crinkling and surrendering without a fight, overwhelmed by the sweat gathering beneath the glistening strands of her Dixie Peach-scented hair.

Five minutes earlier, two white men in a truck had sped up and driven dangerously close to where she stood on the shoulder of the road. The tires missed her feet by a few inches and

3

through the grimy haze of dust the screeching tires raised, Jessie saw the men's sunburned faces and their gaze moving like footsteps across her face. The men sat in the truck, idling the engine, so close to her they could have reached out the window and touched her. They sat there trying to decide whether to drive on or to relieve their boredom by terrorizing her.

When finally they began to drive away, their careening drunken laughter was the only sound, besides Jessie's heart, filling the sun-beaten afternoon. Then a few hundred yards up the road, one of the men leaned out the window on the passenger side and stared back at Jessie, a beer bottle dangling from his hand. The truck began a slow, relentless drive in reverse. Fear rattled in her mind like chains. She was so frightened that she picked up the string-tied cardboard box packed with her clothes and walked in the opposite direction. She kept her eyes downcast, plotting in her mind some form of escape across the flat, endless cotton fields on either side of the highway. The truck's tires rolled across the uneven buckled tar of the road with a soft whine. When she heard the squeal of brakes, she thought her life was over, but a moment later the engine revved up, cranking and irritable. Still Jessie kept walking, not stopping when the strap on her sandal broke. And even when the twine on the box she carried snapped, Jessie retrieved the box from the ground without missing a step. Counting silently, she shoved fear momentarily from her mind. When she reached one hundred Jessie stopped and dared to look behind her. The truck was now only a flicker of red on the distant horizon and she collapsed in relief, falling heavily on the cardboard box. Her heart was pounding, scratching for release like some tiny animal chewing its way out of a trap.

Jessie swallowed a wad of spit, trying to quench a sudden, parching thirst and ran her tongue across her lips. Heat shimmered and danced in waves, as she gazed across the highway.

In her imagination, the sun locked its sweltering hands around her neck. Nausea quickened in the pit of her stomach and in a hot, vivid flash of memory, she felt her father's hands unbuttoning her blouse, cradling her breasts. He had sneaked up on her, like some kind of thief, as she was standing at the stove, turning on the fire beneath the black cast iron frying pan. She had been daydreaming. Daydreaming because Chester Foster's hands couldn't reach her there. Daydreaming to save her life. But then, he was on her like a smell, like a fever, his tongue on her neck, his knee jammed between her legs and his hands holding her breasts, squeezing them so hard that tears welled in the corners of her eyes. And she had whispered, "No, Daddy, please no."

Even now, Jessie couldn't say why yesterday was different. Why yesterday at the moment her father turned her around to face him, she had let her hand reach for the handle of the frying pan, been grateful for its weight, and hit her father on the head once, then again. She didn't know why she had stood there watching him stagger and fall onto the cracked, dull green linoleum of the kitchen floor, before sinking to her knees as solemnly as if to pray, and hit him a third time as he lay in a slick, glistening stream of blood. At the sight of her father's body, monstrous, unmoving, Jessie felt a smile tremble as cautiously as a nervous tick on her lips. Chester Foster wore a pair of blue-striped boxer shorts and a sleeveless undershirt and a stocking cap to protect his pomade-scented waves. Walking down the street, Chester Foster turned his muscular former boxer's build into a taunt. At home he walked around shirtless, his solid body bludgeoning his family into silence and obedience. Now he lay crumpled at his daughter's feet. Jessie couldn't hear him breathing. And she didn't care. The feel of the warm pan handle against her palm had pumped her full of an anger so pure, she never wanted the feeling to end.

The blood began to stain her skirt, and Jessie rose from the floor just as Mae Ann, a bag of groceries in her arms, entered the kitchen. Mae Ann's eyes ballooned in terror and she dropped the bag, cans and jars and boxes crashing around their father's frame.

"What yall done done?" she screamed. Mae Ann's voice wailed, as unsettling and stunning as a siren. That's when Jessie ran.

She went to Aunt Eva's, telling her as she sat in Eva's living room, her arms wrapped around her body as if afraid she would disintegrate if she let herself go, "I did a terrible thing. A terrible thing."

Eva escorted her back home, where Jessie stood trembling with fear on the sidewalk in front of the house, not daring to go in. Eva got her clothes and told her sister, Jessie's mother, Olive, that Jessie said she wasn't coming back. Junior and Willie had stared at her from behind the screen door while Aunt Eva was in the house. Junior gazed at Jessie, from a face that seemed to her to be a blunt, dangerous instrument. Then he turned and walked back into the house, appearing to evaporate in the cool shadows of the hallway. Willie stole quickly down the steps and hugged her, pressing a five-dollar bill in her hand, his light brown eyes whispering good-bye because he did not want to say the words. Mae Ann ran around from the back and grabbed Jessie's hands. "They done took him to the hospital," she told Jessie breathlessly. "He woke up when they put him in the ambulance." Then she begged, "Take me with you, Jess. You cain't be the only one gits away." When Aunt Eva came out to the porch, Mae Ann said to Jessie under her breath, "Send for me, you hear? Send for me," the plea fluttering mournfully, choking Jessie's heart as she watched Mae Ann run to the back of the house.

As Eva and Jessie drove away the sound of Olive Foster's

voice calling Jessie's name again and again drenched the warm night air. Jessie sat straight and still in the front seat, refusing to hear. She would never know that her mother sat on the porch until daybreak praying and waiting for her to come back home. Aunt Eva, who had never married, who owned a small beauty shop, who had been to Atlanta, Memphis and New York with her church, said to Jessie as she spread a sheet on the sofa in the living room that night, "You done sent your daddy to the hospital and I wants to know why." Lighting up a Lucky Strike, her head a field of pink rollers, her lean, angular body swathed in a blue chenille robe, Eva crossed her legs, stared at Jessie and said, "I'm listening. I ain't been your aunt all this time for you to start lying or trying to hold back on me now. What's been going on in that house?"

Jessie answered Eva with a sob so resolute, so complete, that Eva stubbed out her cigarette and reached for Jessie, cradling her in her arms.

"I can't tell nobody. I can't never tell nobody. Not even God," she said. Eva sat on the sofa holding Jessie against her breast until the girl fell into a longed-for but tortured sleep. Three hours before Eva was due home the next afternoon, Jessie packed her things and left.

THE DARK GREEN Ford, one headlight missing, the front fender smashed, its body caked with dust, sputtered toward Jessie in a fog of sun and heat. She stood up, dusted herself off and stepped closer to the highway to see who was driving. Slowly she raised her hand. The car slowed down and stopped right in front of her. Inside the car was a young man with a trace of freckles that mapped his nose and cheeks. Around his mouth were the stubbly beginnings of a beard.

"Where you headed?" he asked, leaning over to the passenger side.

"I'm goin' to Winona, can you gimme a lift that far?"

"You running away from home, ain't you," he grinned, his face more smug than Jessie could bear.

"How come you ask that?"

"You got a running away from home look on your face."

"So what if I am, ain't none a your business," Jessie countered, stepping back quickly from the car.

"I didn't say it was. Come on, I'll give you a lift."

"Where you headed?" Jessie asked, leaning back through the window.

"I'm driving over to Greenwood."

Jessie opened the door and pressed her cardboard box under the dashboard as she settled in the front seat.

"What's your name?" he asked, starting the car.

"Jessie, Jessie Foster."

"Hi, I'm Lincoln Sturgis. What'll you do when you get to Winona?"

"I got some people there, my grandmama. But she don't really know I'm coming."

"So you *are* running away," he laughed.

"I didn't say that. You sure ask a lot of questions," Jessie said, squirming in discomfort beside Lincoln, his curiosity pricking her with guilt. "Where you from?" she asked, turning to look at him. He was lanky, with tributaries of blue veins riddling the light skin of his arms, which seemed burnished by a tan that made him golden and perfect.

"I'm from Montgomery, but I'm headed to Greenwood, to work in the movement."

"The movement? What's that?"

"Ain't you heard, girl? This here is *Freedom Summer*," Lincoln said, a joyous, hearty laugh rumbling in his voice, initiating her, Jessie felt, into a knowledge both frightening and momentous.

"Well, I knew I was gonna get *my* freedom, but I didn't know nobody else had that in mind," she said, trembling a little at this burst of humor, amazed at the sudden comfort she felt, confused by how much she liked looking at Lincoln. She wondered what he saw when he looked at her. "You one of them freedom riders?"

"I've done just about everything else. Picketed segregated stores. Tried to get Negroes to register and vote. Anything to get us our civil rights."

"So, you're a civil rights worker," Jessie said, suddenly flushed with fear, as if he had told her he was a convict on the run from the law.

"You could be one too," he said, his eyes cast upon her with serious intent.

"I'd be too scared."

Six months ago, Alberta Garrison, the daughter of one of the deacons in her mother's church, had gone off to Jackson to protest something to do with civil rights, Jessie recalled. The girl had gotten arrested and nobody had heard from her since. Alberta's best friend, Iola Hughes, had gone to Jackson with her and come back to Columbus and told Alberta's family that Alberta was taken out of her cell one night and never returned. At seventeen, Alberta Garrison sang in the church choir, her luminous contralto never failing to spark a fervent chorus of amens from the congregation. The rest of the week, however, she rebelled against her parents' strict regime at home by cutting school, and having sex with the town's most dangerous young men in the backseat of cars, in rented rooms and in cotton fields. But when Alberta met the civil rights workers who came to town, she changed. Her parents were fearful but proud. Alberta began dressing primly and wouldn't give a boy she didn't know a smile or the time of day. Some people got saved, Alberta got civil rights. And now, nobody knew or wanted to imagine what had happened to her.

And on the plantation where Jessie sometimes picked cotton, one afternoon the boss had driven onto the fields, and ordered all the workers to gather around his pickup truck. In the flatbed where cotton was hauled lay a young Negro, his bleeding, purplish lips swollen, his left eye bloated, sealed shut, the skin of his cheeks slit, the scent of his exposed flesh drawing a family of flies around his head. His hands were tied behind his back. "This here is what civil rights is gonna git anybody what wants em," the boss had shouted. "This boy come around trying to git yall to vote. Well, I just give him a lecture on civil rights he won't never forget." As the man drove off, the field hands stood beneath a suddenly grieving afternoon sun, speech bleeding in their throats. Jessie had seen a reprise of the young man's face for weeks afterward when she read a schoolbook, looked out the window or stared at the sky.

"Hell, I'm scared too," she heard Lincoln say, his admission yanking her from the hold of memory. "But I'm more scared of things staying the way they are. What about your family? Won't they miss you?"

"I hope so," Jessie said, turning away from Lincoln to gaze out the window, "I really do."

In the backseat were several boxes filled with manuscripts, poems and plays that Lincoln told Jessie he had written. While driving, he recited lines from *King Lear* and *Hamlet*, and told her he was working in the movement, so he could be set on fire and "write an anthem for our people."

Lincoln made this pronouncement so passionately that Jessie knew he took the extraordinary for granted. She had never known anyone to talk like that. Her parents spoke as little as

10

possible, as though speech would merely enhance their misery. Growing up in the grip of silence, Jessie's head had nonetheless teemed with words. Her father had warned her never to tell. Her mother had said over and over, "I don't want to hear nothing about that man, or what he's done." In her house words were contraband, proscribed. Jessie had craved words all the more because they were forbidden. Her daydreams persistent, resilient, consisted mostly of scenes in which happy people talked on and on as though the act of speech were a saving grace.

She had seen the Bullocks, the white family she cleaned house for three days a week after school, sit as though hypnotized by their black and white television set. The words and laughter and jokes and stories just coming at them. Walter Cronkite telling them the news, Red Skelton making them laugh. Jessie had watched them gather around the television set like it was an altar. She knew it was words that brought them in front of the screen.

Lincoln talked nonstop. His vigorous, confident energy affirmed Jessie's daydreams, and satisfied a hunger she had grown used to feeling. One minute Lincoln was imitating Sammy Davis, Jr., the next telling Jessie that President Kennedy was killed by people high up in the government. He recited parts of the U.S. Constitution and told her about some New York preacher whose last name was X who Jessie hadn't heard anything about.

But she *had* heard about the Freedom Riders who had ridden interstate buses across the south to integrate them. Negro men and women getting on the buses and sitting wherever they wanted, not just in the back where first the law and then custom said they had to sit. Negroes standing in the white section of the bus station waiting rooms, drinking from the water fountains marked "white only."

There were white Freedom Riders, Jessie knew that. And all

of them were being beaten by mobs and jailed. The colored folks in Columbus couldn't stop talking about the Freedom Riders and the whites couldn't invent curses bad enough for them. The Negro preachers in Columbus said special prayers for them on Sundays and took up collections to help bail them out of jail. The sheriffs of towns and cities across the deep south had sworn to shoot any Freedom Rider, Negro or white, who set foot in their town.

Jessie had watched this fevered push toward freedom from afar, as though she was a spectator at a play, fascinated by the action on stage, unconvinced of its relevance to her.

"I bet you been to college," Jessie said, throwing her arm across the back of the seat, turning so she could just look at Lincoln all the time if she wanted.

"Yeah, Miles College over in Birmingham."

"Then how come you ain't lookin for a job?"

"Some things are more important than a job."

"Like what?" Jessie asked incredulously. Never in her life had she heard anybody say such a thing.

"Like the right to vote. Like being able to have the same rights as everybody else," Lincoln said, his voice urgent, his face animated, turning his glance from the road to look at Jessie as he spoke.

"You mean white folks?" she asked. "From what I seen, I don't want to be like them."

"No, but I want the same rights they have," Lincoln said emphatically. "You see what we did in Montgomery with the bus boycott."

"Vote gonna git us better jobs?" Jessie asked skeptically, thinking about her mother's demeaning work as a domestic, her father's meager salary as a janitor for a funeral home and the need for herself, Willie and Junior and Mae Ann to pick cotton to make extra needed money.

"That's what the vote is for," Lincoln said.

Jessie leaned forward and turned on the radio.

"Don't work," Lincoln told her. They were nearing Winona. The endless flatness of the land with only an occasional house or store was giving way to small clusters of gas stations and restaurants. The sun was now a deep orange slash across the evening sky.

"You ever wonder why God made it so hard for us colored?" Jessie asked wistfully.

"God didn't do that. White men did."

"But you really think we're good enough?" Jessie pressed him. "For equal rights I mean. You know what they say bout us, that we're in our rightful place." Jessie wondered if Lincoln could hear in her voice how many times she had thought that was true, how often she had swallowed it whole, lived on the belief as if it were the bread of life.

"They're wrong about us, Jessie. Always been wrong. We're gonna set the record straight," he said, squeezing her hands reassuringly as they lay folded in her lap.

What was she running from? Lincoln wondered. That Jessie was a runaway signaled courage as well as desperation. Her body was firm and mature. He could tell from the condition of her hands, arms and legs that she had worked hard and, of necessity, all her short life. But dimples appeared in her cheeks when she laughed and her eyes were large, clear and honest against the ruddy brown of her face. But those eyes had a furtive edge too, as though they held lethal secrets. Lincoln, who was already beginning to think of himself as a writer, figured secrets made a person more interesting. He knew that everything he saw, touched, learned, felt, would be transformed into words on a page. So what did secrets mean? How could he fear his secrets or anyone else's when he could change them into anything he imagined or desired.

The girls he had left behind in Montgomery and Birmingham snubbed him because he was an orphan, or listened politely to his poetry and whispered behind his back that he was queer. Talking to those girls he had everything to prove and everything to lose. But when Lincoln began working with the Student Nonviolent Coordinating Committee, SNCC, as it was popularly known, the same girls wanted to go out with him because nobody knew if he would live long enough to see the "freedom" he talked so much about, or be dredged from some tributary of the Mississippi River. The hint of possible sudden danger, the knowledge of his obvious courage, made him a marked man. More than one young woman wanted to be able to say that *she* was the last one who had held Lincoln Sturgis alive in her arms.

But he could tell Jessie was different. He liked looking at her, just sitting beside her. Conversation with her was not a bloodletting but a kind of communion. He realized it was going to be hard to say good-bye.

"Why don't you come on to Greenwood with me?" he asked. "There's plenty of work to do."

"I told you, I'm scared."

"I told you I was too."

"I don't even *know* you," Jessie protested.

"Well, I don't know you either, but I know you don't belong in Winona."

Jessie searched Lincoln's face for something she could mistrust, some flicker in his eyes, some movement of his lips that would inform her that she was in danger. And when she didn't find it, Jessie thought of her grandma Bessie. She was running to her only because she'd always been the old woman's favorite. But then she remembered the newspaper lining the walls of her grandmama's two-room shack on the outskirts of the city, the old woman's hard life of survival on welfare and handouts from a family for whom she had once been a nanny. And what would she do in Winona? Hardly any white businesses would hire a Negro, even one with a high school diploma.

They had entered Winona, and Lincoln stopped at a gas station and filled the tank. Then he drove farther into town and parked in the commercial district and said to Jessie, "I'm not pressuring you, I'm just offering you the chance to do something that matters."

"Where you gonna stay?"

"There's a house set up for the movement people."

"What about me?"

"You'd stay there too. I bet you'd have your own room."

She had been trying to get away from 468 Davis Road as long as she could remember. It was a street whose tiny frame houses huddled together like heads bowed to avoid being slapped. There were outhouses in some backyards. Peeling, crumbling wood defaced most of the exteriors. In the summertime, the street's young men gathered on the corners like conspirators thrusting their voices into the seams of the night. Voices desperate to be heard. Desperate not to be ignored. On Davis Road nobody believed in the possibility of civil rights. Nobody even knew what they were. That was the street where everyone had watched the sheriff's deputy pay regular visits to Elvira McCullough. Everyone sitting on the front stoops remembered the spring evenings when they would see Mr. McCullough walk toward his house, spot the now familiar police car parked out front, and turn away and head toward Bo Willie's juke joint, where he would get drunk and wait for the white man to leave.

And in her house Jessie had always been lonely. Then she had learned to be afraid. Afraid of white men. Afraid of her father. Because she knew so well the feeling of fear, she knew when she was safe.

15

She sat twisting the hem of her skirt, her back to Lincoln's persistent, kind, impatient gaze. Finally he said, "Come on, girl, you just running in circles. At least we know where I'm headed," and started up the car.

A MILE OUTSIDE of Carol, Lincoln's car shuddered to a halt. He turned the engine on repeatedly. But nothing happened. He and Jessie walked back to town and found a Negro mechanic who drove them back to the car. After looking at the engine he told them the alternator was shot and that he could repair it but not until the next morning. "I got a wake to go to tonight."

THEY REGISTERED in the rooming house as Mr. and Mrs. Brown. Jessie stood nervously behind Lincoln, his gym bag and boxes of books and papers, her cardboard box, now near total collapse, stationed around her feet like unwashed, unruly children of whom she was ashamed. As Lincoln signed the registry, the elderly woman behind the desk, tall, angular, white-haired, looked at Jessie through narrowed, censorious eyes. Then she led them upstairs to the second floor, saying, "No cooking in the rooms, no loud music after ten o'clock, and yall have to check out by noon or I charge for another day."

The pink and white wallpaper was water-stained and dingy, its tiny white flowers as cheerless and abused as the chipped and scratched desk and the three-legged table at the foot of the bed. Last year's calendar from a local funeral home and a tiny framed picture of Jesus ascending to heaven graced the walls.

"There ain't but one bed," Jessie said after Lincoln had brought their bags and boxes up to the room.

"How bout that," he said, scanning the room quickly, then dismissing it.

"I'll sleep on the floor," he told Jessie, sitting down beside her on the bed, which was covered by a spread whose washed-out, faded colors vainly attempted to match the wallpaper.

"Well, that ain't fair."

"Yes, it is. Don't worry. I've slept in worse places. . . . I'm gonna go get us something to eat. I saw a place on the corner."

When Jessie heard the front door close on the first floor, she ran to the window and watched Lincoln walk toward the tiny corner restaurant that advertised barbecue and chitlins. Lincoln moved like a man who knew where he was going, but didn't need to hurry to get there, Jessie thought, watching him nod politely to the people he passed. Turning from the window to once again face the room, she decided not to think about what she had done—wounded her father, run away, hitched a ride with a stranger, checked into a rooming house to spend the night with him, with plans to wake up in the morning to go off and do things that could get her arrested, beaten or killed. No, she decided, a shiver seizing her, threatening to unsettle the contentment she had fashioned from the cloth of this day. She wouldn't think about any of that now.

By the time Lincoln returned, Jessie had bathed, had dressed in clean clothes and lined their boxes neatly against the wall. They ate fried-fish sandwiches and french fries spread out on the tiny desk. Then Lincoln went to take a bath, while Jessie cleared away the remnants of their meal. But the sound of water filling the tub, Lincoln flushing the toilet, his rich baritone humming "Amazing Grace," made Jessie so nervous that she decided it wasn't proper for her to stay in the room with only an unlocked door separating her from a naked man she didn't know. She couldn't bear the thought of sitting in the front room, under the landlady's disapproving gaze. So Jessie sat on the steps outside their door.

When she entered the room Lincoln had made a pallet on the floor, using blankets he'd found in the closet. He wore a tee shirt and a pair of old pajama bottoms. Jessie claimed the bed, scurrying beneath the covers fully dressed.

"You gonna be awful hot sleeping in your clothes," Lincoln laughed.

"You just let me worry bout that, Lincoln Sturgis."

"You gonna tell me why you're running away?" he asked, stretched out on the floor, gazing up at Jessie.

"Maybe one day I will."

Lincoln turned on his back and said, "I used to run away too. But I wasn't running away from home, I was running to try and find one."

Then in a quiet, dispassionate voice, almost as though he were talking about someone else's life, Lincoln told Jessie who he was. His parents were killed in an automobile accident when he was three and for the next six years he was shunted between the homes of relatives unable or unwilling to care for him. Finally he was put in a Negro orphanage. Lincoln was a gregarious, quick-witted boy who, in order to survive, had learned to read people like books. The head administrator, J. R. Sturgis, took a liking to him and adopted him. While Sturgis treated Lincoln with affection and concern, the boy was never fully accepted by Sturgis's wife and two sons. When J. R. Sturgis died of a heart attack in Lincoln's junior year at Miles College, his wife cut off support for Lincoln's studies, and denied him the money his adoptive father had left him.

"So you ain't got no family, to speak of?" Jessie said quietly, wondering how that felt.

18

"Not since J. R. Sturgis died."

"Don't you git lonely though, for brothers and sisters?" Jessie asked, hungering in the wake of the question to see Mae Ann, Willie and Junior. She looked at Lincoln's long legs stretched out before him. She marveled at his big feet, almost pink, not tan like the rest of him. Jessie wondered if he could see, on her face, hear in her voice, the things that had been done to her. The things she'd never told.

The sound of several cars speeding down the street, a woman's luxurious squealing laughter, a mother calling Re-gi-naaaaaald, come on in, floated in the window. Together they listened, silent, at ease.

After a while, Jessie heard Lincoln say, "You just don't think about what you never had. About how you been hurt."

He was wrong, saying that. She knew you never forgot. She had graduated from high school three weeks earlier, and she had begun to wonder more and more why all the older people she knew, the ones she was supposed to look up to, lived, it seemed, on lies.

"How'd you get into this civil rights stuff anyway?" she asked, hugging her pillow, stretching out, waiting to hear Lincoln tell her something she would never forget.

"Well, I didn't study it in school," he laughed. "I just started working with friends of mine from other colleges—boycotting, picketing, trying to get people to register and vote. The only family I got now is movement folks."

"What if I don't do good? What if they don't like me where we goin?" Jessie asked.

"The minute you arrive in town, you pass the most important test," he told her. "Then all you got to do is keep showing up, the next day and the day after that."

"You make it sound so easy."

"It is when you realize there's nowhere you can go until you straighten up things where you are."

Lincoln turned off the light and said good night. When she knew he was asleep, Jessie removed her skirt and blouse and slipped on her robe. Around three o'clock she woke up and felt Lincoln beside her in the bed. In sleep, his body was tense, poised, Jessie thought, for flight, ready to leave nothing behind. His arms greedily hugged the pillow. Jessie could feel the melancholy sadness of his dreams whispering in the darkened room. She watched him sleep for a few minutes and then lay back down. In the dark, with her back to him, she touched Lincoln's arm, absorbed the rise and fall of his frame, his craggy labored breathing inside her hand. Then she quickly pulled her hand away. Tomorrow was almost here.

GREENWOOD SAT on the muddy, silent banks of the Yazoo River, surrounded by Itta Bena, Moorhead, Sidon, Pew City. Here, the circumference of the whole world was measured by the boundaries of the cotton field. The Mississippi Delta stretched from Vicksburg to Memphis, two hundred miles of flat, fertile terrain. A million black hands, working from dawn to dusk, decade after decade, had planted and harvested "King Cotton." Change had come once in the form of the Emancipation Proclamation and curdled into a bitter illusion. Now, a revolution reverberated across the Delta and Greenwood was the crossroads. Reality was becoming legend even as it happened—Sam Block and Willie Peacock coming to town to canvas for black voters, and because they had no car, riding around Greenwood on a mule. Jimmy Travis shot in the neck and almost killed, while driving on Highway 82 with two other movement workers. The bullet didn't kill Jimmy or the push to get the vote.

In the Freedom House that summer, Jessie heard jazz for the first time, saw a white woman naked and sat down to eat beside a white man. She shared a room with Carolyn Seavers, from Minnesota, one of hundreds of northern college students who had come to the Delta to help register black voters.

Carolyn's blond hair hung to her waist and her blue eyes were the color of the sky just after a good hard rain. The first time Jessie saw her, Jessie was sitting in the tiny bedroom she had been given, waiting for Lincoln to come back and take her to a church where she would begin teaching adults to read and write, when Carolyn suddenly entered the room carrying a small suitcase. "Hi, my name's Carolyn," she said, walking up to Jessie and extending her hand. Her smile wrapped itself around Jessie and lifted her from the bed. Carolyn's presence filled the room with the feel of something tangible, powerful, Jessie thought. It was the same room that had felt dormant, inert, only moments before. Jessie looked at Carolyn's hand— the nails, neat, perfectly manicured—a hand so soft and un- blemished that to Jessie it didn't look real. She saw the green birthstone ring on the middle finger, and stubbornly hid her own hands behind her back. No white woman had ever wanted to touch her. Mrs. Bullock slapped her once because she had broken an expensive piece of china, and then turned and wiped her hand on a nearby towel as if she were afraid Jessie was contagious. And here this white girl stood, pushing her hand in Jessie's face.

"I'm Jessie Foster," she said, her voice weak, small, dimin- ished by the blondness, the whiteness, the pinkness, of the girl who stood before her.

"Well," Carolyn said, dropping her hand, turning hurt and confused away from Jessie, "looks like we're roommates."

While Carolyn unpacked her things, Jessie sat quietly on the bed with her back to her. When Lincoln knocked on the door, she ran from the room so fast she nearly fell over Carolyn, kneeling on the floor unpacking her clothes.

That evening, around a table laden with pots and plates of food donated by neighbors, Carolyn turned to Jessie and told her, "Call me Cate, that's what I go by for short." Jessie stared at her as though the floor lamp had just spoken and nodded, quickly mustering a halting, "Sure, I'll do that." The black and white faces crowded around the table struck Jessie as some perverse, dangerous rainbow. The aggressive friendliness of the northern college students confused and then confounded her. During dinner Jessie heard Odetta and Joan Baez for the first time, their songs filling the room from a tiny portable record player someone had brought. Baez's lush, pure voice struck Jessie as so perfect, it almost stopped her heart. And Odetta transformed the story, the history, the face, of everybody she already knew, into a thing of majestic glory. When they finished eating, Lincoln read several of his poems, hushing the room's edgy self-conscious excitement with language that was as resonant as the songs they had just heard. Jessie listened intently, hearing all the things that Lincoln hadn't stopped thinking about, although he'd told her he had. When Lincoln finished, Jessie spotted Carolyn talking to Marlon Jeeter, a slender young man, so dark that when Jessie looked at him, she shivered. His black skin held not the slightest hint of dilution. Although quite young, Marlon sported a beard, already flecked with strands of gray. Carolyn sat next to him, her laughter spinning concentric circles around their intent, her knee occasionally touching his, shaking her mane of blond hair repeatedly, the way Jessie had seen white girls do in the movies. Lincoln and Hamilton Schwartz, a student from New Jersey, had begun a game of chess at the dinner table.

What Jessie sat witnessing was such a mockery of everything she had been taught, she was almost afraid to continue looking. The Freedom House was alien territory, a foreign country lodged in the solid hard heart of Mississippi. Jessie didn't know if she could learn to speak the language required on this soil. And the fear that she could not made her jittery and headachy and suddenly so afraid that she ran onto the porch and sat on the steps. Here, finally, she could breathe.

Moments later, Lincoln joined her and asked, "What's wrong?"

"I ain't never in my life seen nothing like what's going on in there," she told him, shaking her head in disbelief, terrified of even glancing back over her shoulder into the living room. "Everybody all mixed up together. Like color don't matter," she whispered breathlessly, terrified of even saying out loud what her eyes had seen and refused to believe.

"That's what the movement's about," he said gently.

"I thought we was just gonna register people to vote."

"We are. But that's gonna change everything, Jessie, everything."

That night in bed beside Carolyn, Jessie hugged the edge of the mattress, so fearful was she of touching the girl who slept in only a bra and panties.

She heard Carolyn stir. In response Jessie moved closer to the edge of the bed, her nails digging into the soft round edges of the old mattress, her hips, back, stomach, all sucked in to make her small and unobtrusive. The room was humid. The air outside the window was still, unmoving. A mosquito buzzed around Jessie's ear. Carolyn had turned on her side and Jessie felt the warmth of her breath on her neck as she said, "My parents would die if they knew I was here. They think I'm in New York." The girl's voice was giddy, glazed with excitement and dread as she waited for Jessie's response.

Jessie felt a moment of empathy and wondered if Carolyn Seavers had run away from home too.

"They wouldn't give me permission to come down here. So I told them I was going to visit a friend in Rye, New York. Can you believe it, Jessie, they dared me to come. They don't let me do anything," Carolyn complained, turning on her back. "They shelter me all the time, from life, from reality." Carolyn spoke in that blunt, energetic, fully self-possessed way characteristic of the northern college students. They talked, Jessie thought, as though words were invented just for them. And the words Jessie heard them use were hard, abstract words that they could command like a toy, or play with like a game.

"Did your parents do that to you, Jessie, you know, keep you from having experiences?" The girl's voice was genuinely distraught, and in it Jessie could hear all the arguments, the crying and the screaming that went on in the nice big house Carolyn Seavers had left in Minneapolis.

But what, Jessie wondered, did Carolyn mean by experiences? Did that mean living, the things you went through every day, the stuff you had to put up with, couldn't get away from no matter what? Or did that mean something different? Something you decided you wanted and then went out and did.

Jessie didn't know and so she said reassuringly, "I think you'll get a lot of experience this summer, Carolyn. When you go back home you'll have plenty to tell."

But restless, unsatisfied by Jessie's words, Carolyn left their bed, to sit by the window and smoke a cigarette. Watching Carolyn's profile cast against the window, highlighted by the glow of the moon, Jessie wondered what it took for white people to be happy. They had claimed all the beauty and goodness in the world and wrapped themselves up in it. With none left for anybody else. And just like Carolyn Seavers, that still wasn't enough. Carolyn sat there for a long time, quiet, but agitated, Jessie could tell, before suddenly asking, "I guess you're used to being scared, huh?" her voice easily intruding, poring over the outline of Jessie's life. Jessie wondered how she knew, how this white girl from the north knew.

"What you mean?" she asked, suddenly terrified, her head bobbing up in the darkness.

"I mean, you know, the lynchings and the Klan and the way you guys can't vote."

"Oh, that's what you mean?" Every pore on her body was instantly bathed in relief. Resting her head again on the pillow, Jessie wanted to laugh and to cry.

"What did you think I meant?" Carolyn asked, blowing a thin stream of smoke out the window.

Jessie smiled grimly in the darkness and said, "Nothing. I was just thinking about something else, that's all."

"I guess it's pretty bad for you down here," Carolyn insisted. Her voice felt to Jessie like hands rubbing her, touching her, trespassing.

"It ain't all bad all the time," she heard herself say. "You'd be surprised how long I can go without thinking about rednecks or white folks not liking me."

"I just don't see how you guys have stood it all this time, all these years," Carolyn marveled, mashing out the cigarette in a small ashtray and folding her arms across her chest.

"You talk like we're mules or something," Jessie said, a completely new, hard anger seizing her with the desire to throw something at Carolyn Seavers. "We're folks just like you. And there's been plenty of us fighting back. Long before yall come here." Jessie did not know this as fact. But she knew it as an instinctive, total truth.

"I didn't mean it the way it sounded," Carolyn sighed, walking back to the bed. She lay down beside Jessie and whispered good night.

In the dark, Jessie waited for Carolyn's breathing to grow shallow, regular. Then she propped herself up on an elbow and stared at the jumbled mass of golden, silky hair cascading over Carolyn's pillow. This was hair that Jessie had pretended she possessed standing before the living room mirror as a child, scarves draped over her head. More than once she had wished so hard for hair like this that she had opened her eyes and yes, yes, there it was surrounding her dark face. The hair had vanished in the blink of an eye, but she *had* wished it, made it so. She reached out and touched Carolyn's hair, gently at first and then possessively, feeling its texture, its weight, the way the long strands curled at the end. Jessie had wondered so long at the sight of hair like this, fantasized about its feel, that beneath her hands it was suddenly a disappointment—light, thin, insubstantial. Still, Jessie felt reassured for the first time that day. She closed her eyes, silently stroking Carolyn Seaver's hair until she fell asleep.

SHE HAD FINALLY taught the man to write his name. The white lined paper was crinkled, smudged and as tortured as the trembling, frail script that spelled out Bob McGee. The man, who, when Jessie had asked his age, told her, "I'm near bout old as dirt," had struggled with the cursive, looping script for nearly two weeks, practicing the letters of the alphabet, then words as simple as cat and dog, before moving to words that defined and shaped his life—cotton, tractor, his name. So proud was he of the letters that filled the page in a grimy but sturdy pattern that he strutted around the long table and shoved his paper beneath the glance of the other adults who sat sounding out vowels, reading simple sentences from first-grade primers, and writing the first letters of their lives to friends and family.

"Oh, sit yo self down, Bob McGee, Odessa Pendergast yelled

in mock exasperation. "You ain't the only one in this room know how to read and write. You ain't the only one gonna git to vote."

The school, held in the basement of Faith Rising Baptist Church, held classes from nine in the morning until eight at night. In the morning, the children came, ragtag, unwashed, some with hungry, bloated bellies poking through holes in their shirts and dresses. In the evening, the adults arrived, straight from jobs or dinner. Working with these people made Jessie miss her family and she wondered when she would see them again. One night after all her students had gone, she wrote a letter to her sister, Mae Ann.

Dear Mae Ann:

I don't know when I'll be able to send for you like you asked. But I am safe and have met a nice man who really likes me and treats me good. We are someplace nearby doing important work that's gonna help us all live the way we was meant to. Don't worry about me. I am safe. I am afraid but not really scared, like I used to be. I am helping to fight for freedom.

Love,
Jessie

"The irony of all this is that without the vote we count for nothing, absolutely nothing. But if the vote is all we get, it don't, by itself, mean didley squat." Courtland Hightower spat out the words with a weary shake of his shaved head, his brown eyes tense and restless prowling Lincoln's face.

"That doesn't matter now, not to these people. They're taking a walk to the courthouse to register and that may be the bravest thing they've ever done," Lincoln said.

"Always the idealist," Courtland laughed, leaning back in his chair and plucking a toothpick out of the pocket of his overalls. His laughter slid easily between the two men, like a balm. "I didn't say voting doesn't count, I said we're in danger of canon-izing the act. Hell, the people that really run this country prob-ably haven't voted in years, decades. No, they just determine which of *their* lackeys we choose."

"I'm not arguing with your reasoning I'm just declaring it irrelevant," Lincoln said, leaning close to Courtland, his face lit by an impish grin that savored the verbal joust the two friends had launched nearly an hour before.

"You hear that, Jessie, the boy done turned pro-found on me, declared me irrelevant. White folks have called me nigger, women called me dog, friends called me fool, but this hurts more than all those put together. Irrelevant."

Jessie sat watching Courtland and Lincoln poring over a map of Mississippi spread out on the cracked, wobbly card ta-ble in the living room of the Freedom House. They had finished a meager dinner of black-eyed peas and corn bread and when Jessie cleared the table Courtland spread out the map and be-gan dotting it with red stars to mark areas where voter regis-tration programs were in place. She had sat listening to the two men, as she often did, soaking up information, ideas, the meaning of what she found herself in the midst of. When she first met Courtland, Jessie could hardly stop staring at his head—shaved, gleaming with perspiration. It seemed to Jessie a kind of crystal ball that was home to his subversive, mili-tantly expressed thoughts. One day, catching Jessie staring at him, Courtland had said, "I guess you wonder why I cut off all my hair. I can think better this way." He'd pointed to Lincoln, who sat beside him in the truck they were riding in, "Now you take a man like Lincoln, all that hair he's got, no won-der he can't think straight." And then he had laughed, his broad chest shuddering, his usually solemn face alive with merriment.

Lincoln and Courtland had slept on the floors of sharecroppers' houses in Alabama, sneaking off plantations before the sun came up. They had slept in a pickup truck as they made their way halfway across the state of Georgia, being fed by families who wanted to help as the two men searched for towns where they could work with local people. They had been afraid together, had been jailed together and when she watched them, Jessie felt a force of friendship join them like a silent, tough cord.

Lincoln had taken Jessie out with him that day, canvassing for voters and children for the Freedom Schools. Driving along the back roads, Jessie asked Lincoln to stop wherever they saw children's clothes hung up on clotheslines in the back.

At some houses, the tenants refused to let them in. Women stood fearful and mute behind partially opened doors as Lincoln or Jessie asked if they'd register to vote, assuring them that they could take classes to prepare. When Jessie asked if they would send their children to the Freedom Schools, some told her harshly, "We ain't got no chil'ren here," even as she saw small hands tugging at the sides of the mothers' dresses or saw curious, eager boys and girls walking down the dirt paths toward the house. They were chased away from one house by an elderly man who threw stones at them and shouted, "Somebody's gonna git kilt, then I guess yall be satisfied. Go on away from here and leave well enough alone."

"You say the vote doesn't count for as much as we think. But it sure as hell counts when we *don't* vote," Lincoln said.

"No doubt about that, no doubt," Courtland conceded. "I'm just concerned about definitions. What we're really talking about, what nobody wants to say, is that we want power. Not just the damn vote, but the power that's supposed to go along with it. But you say power and whites go crazy. You say vote they just get scared."

"How tough you think it's gonna get?" Jessie asked quietly. "I've been hearing about the bombings and shootings in the other counties where registration is going on."

"It's gonna get real tough, Jessie," Courtland said, his fingers entwined, hands flat on his chest. He told her this with a confidence that drove Jessie's eyes from his face to her hands, nervous and twisted in her lap.

"How you come to be in the movement?" Jessie asked Courtland, longing to hear him tell her something that would ease her fear, fill her with the boundless courage she imagined he possessed.

"You ever see a picture of Emmett Till?" Courtland asked her.

"You mean the boy that got lynched?"

"Yeah."

"I heard about it. But I never saw no pictures."

"Well, I *heard* about him and we *talked* about it in my school. And then one day I saw a picture of his body. I saw what you look like after somebody shoots you in the head, crushes your skull and ties a cotton gin fan around your neck before throwing you into the Tallahatchie River where you stay at the bottom for three days. I used to dream about Emmett Till," he said, his voice pinched by pain at the memory, his eyes closing suddenly, quickly, as if to prevent the resurgence of the dream. "I was the same age as him when it happened. I'd go to sleep at night and he'd be sitting at the edge of my bed, his body all bloody and mangled. He was a corpse. He never said a word. Just sat there staring at me. Got so I was scared to go to sleep. Scared to wake up. Dreaming about Emmett Till taught me I could be killed just like him. Not because I tried to vote or to eat at a segregated counter, but just because I was black. I don't dream about him anymore. But I haven't forgotten."

Listening to Lincoln's friend, Jessie had learned that anger did not always have to be checked. Anger could transform, invigorate. Angry, you did things everybody said you couldn't and you thought you never would. But you couldn't get angry until you started thinking. That was the worst part, thinking about the wrong you'd been done. But you couldn't move without it. Sometimes at night in bed, thoughts rampaged through Jessie's mind. Some days she felt herself growing out of her skin.

Jailed eighteen times for leading demonstrations, picketing or just for getting on some sheriff's nerves, Courtland came into a room and filled it up the way white men did, Jessie thought. Watching him lead meetings or plan strategy excited her, made her feel the kind of fear that moves you toward something instead of away.

"When's Macon due back?" Lincoln asked, moving to the sofa to sit beside Jessie, throwing his arm across her shoulder because he could see how much she needed, at this moment, his touch.

"I go pick her up at the airport tomorrow afternoon. I talked to her last night. She said the Quakers in Philadelphia and the Unitarians in New York made impressive contributions after her speeches. I'm going over to see my mother," he told them, rising and stretching his arms and back. "To let her know I'm still alive."

"I'VE GOT SOMETHING for you," Lincoln told Jessie when they were alone, moving closer to her, squeezing her shoulders and kissing her lightly on the cheek. He went upstairs to his room and returned with a large box wrapped in newspaper and tied with string. He handed it to Jessie saying, "Go on, open it."

"What is it?"

"You'll find out."

Inside the box was a pair of blue jeans overalls, the kind that had been adopted as the unofficial uniform of the movement.

"I know that ten dollars a week we get isn't much and those skirts you been wearing don't seem real practical to me."

"Why, Lincoln, I sure do thank you, I really do," Jessie said, blushing happily. "How'd you know my size?"

"I asked Carolyn."

Jessie reached for Lincoln's hand and he leaned over and kissed her.

"I know I pressured you to come, Jessie, but I hope I don't have to pressure you to stay."

"You won't have to do no such thing, Lincoln, not at all. I'm here now cause I want to be. At first I was just here cause I didn't know what else to do."

Lincoln lay his head on Jessie's shoulder and she felt his body wired and tense, warm with a relentless trembling.

"Lincoln, what's wrong?"

"I feel like a twig that's gonna break in two, sometimes," he whispered.

The air of the large, unkempt living room of the Freedom House with its musty used sofa and unmatched chairs was heavy with the evening's sultry heat. Jessie heard her stomach rumble. She was still hungry. The black-eyed peas and corn bread were all she had eaten that day. The noisy, clanking refrigerator in the kitchen was nearly always empty. And they lived on a combination of handouts from neighbors, vegetables picked from the garden in back of the house and free meals sometimes at Booker's Place. Still, Jessie had never been as hungry in her life.

"You don't look like you getting much sleep at night," Jessie said, her hands stroking Lincoln's face, her fingers outlining the dark circles around his eyes.

"I don't," he admitted, holding her fingers, kissing them gently.

"What you worried about?"

"Everything. I've just got a bad feeling. Like something terrible's gonna happen."

"But there's been terrible things happening to us all along."

"I mean in a different way though, a way I can't explain. A way I'm afraid to even think about."

"Thanks for the overalls," Jessie said, eager to change the subject.

"Jessie, I feel responsible for you. Tell me anything you need."

"One day, Lincoln, I'm gonna do that," Jessie promised. "One day I will."

MACON WANTED to pull the phone out of the wall. Every fifteen minutes since midnight, the phone had rung, the neurotic, edgy sound seeming to suck all the air out of the room. The voice promised to make it real tight for niggers and nigger lovers, said a bomb had been planted where they'd never find it (although the entire house and area around it had been searched and nothing was found). Macon never got used to the calls and wondered how Courtland could sleep as he did, so easily beside her.

That morning she and Lincoln had driven over to McComb to investigate the site of a bombed church where voter registration classes had been held. Then when they arrived back in Greenwood, they bailed Courtland out of jail, where he had spent two days on a trumped-up traffic violation, designed to get him off the streets. Every time Macon told Courtland good-bye she never knew if she would see him again. Their existence was charged, live-wire hot with the threat of death, the opportunity to find in themselves the kind of courage no one ever told them they had. They never knew when one of them might be arrested, or when they would have to travel to some far-flung part of the state or region. Macon had never been so afraid of dying, nor had she ever felt so alive.

When she first laid eyes on Courtland Hightower, he was giving a talk in one of her classes at Bennett College in Greensboro, North Carolina. As a junior she had picketed the city's Woolworth's for integrated lunch counters, leading a group of young women in a rowdy march from the sedate campus of the all-girl's school into downtown. In high school she had joined the NAACP youth league and, during summers back home in Richmond, she had walked picket lines outside segregated businesses with her mother and father.

Macon Fields spoke her first full sentence at six months, read her first book at two, in elementary school she skipped two grades. While she had absorbed a bristling sense of the world's enduring injustice from her parents' political activism, she possessed the thoughtful demeanor of a woman who had considered more than once giving up on the world.

Before leading the march on Woolworth's, Macon had been put on probation for initiating a prayer vigil on the steps of the chapel in support of the students sitting in at the five and dime, who had ketchup and mustard poured on their heads by angry mobs and who had been slapped and punched. Because of the fervor of her politics, during three years at Bennett, Macon averaged one date a semester. Her studious, intense eyes

convinced the young men she knew that they were either un-
worthy or too stupid to deserve her attention. So when Macon
heard Courtland address her American History class about the
work he was doing, she was amazed to find that she felt the
first stirrings of sexual desire. "You are intelligent and sensi-
tive," her mother, an English professor who specialized in the
work of Elizabeth Barrett Browning, the Brontë sisters and
Mary Shelley, often told Macon, "and that's worth more than
beauty. Hold on to yourself, your essence," her mother told her,
"until you are in the presence of a man who can match it."
Macon had never met anyone who loomed as large in her imagination, who by word and deed seemed as expansive as Courtland Hightower. And so, she was convinced he was the man her
mother had counseled her to wait for.

After he spoke to her class, Macon got Courtland's address
from her history professor. She wrote him letters in which she
informed him of civil rights activity in the state and asked him
for advice about her studies and her future. She typed the letters, afraid her handwriting would reveal her feelings, and sent
them to his mother's house in Greenwood. Never once did it
occur to Macon that Courtland would not respond. Several
months after his talk at Bennett, Courtland visited his mother
and was handed a small pile of envelopes addressed to him.
The white business envelopes, the typed address on the letters,
all made Courtland wonder who he owed money, who was after
him now, so official did the correspondence seem. Reading in
amazement through half a dozen letters that veered from the
political to the emotional sometimes in the same sentence,
Courtland simply couldn't remember the girl. He wondered if
she might be crazy or dangerous, for in the last letter sent, she
had written, "Courtland Hightower, I love you and know in my
heart that we are destined to be together." Courtland thought
he had seen everything. But those letters so amazed him that

he borrowed money from his mother and caught the next train to North Carolina. When he found Macon's dormitory and sat waiting in the lobby for her, he had no idea who he was waiting for or even why. He hadn't been with a woman in months, so mobile and tenuous was his existence. And suddenly he was getting provocative, strangely irresistible letters from some college student and traveling halfway across the south to find out who she was and why she was proposing what sounded like marriage. When Macon walked into the lobby Courtland remembered her. Four months ago she sat with her eyes riveted to him, and asked several questions about strategy and activism he now remembered thinking were brilliant.

Today she wore a starched man's shirt, blue jeans and her hair was combed back from her face, plain, simple, not crowded in a mass of curls like before. She looked at him as if she'd known he was coming.

"I've been waiting for you to come back since the day you left," she told Courtland, sliding into an overstuffed armchair directly facing him.

"How'd you know I'd come?" he asked, a fleeting anger playing at the edges of his feelings in the face of the girl's certainty.

"You had no choice," she whispered seriously, cupping her chin in her hands.

"Wait a minute now," he protested, nearly rising from the chair.

"Neither did I," she said, standing up, walking toward him as though she'd been doing it all her life.

Macon stood before Courtland and reached for his hands, saying, "I'm glad you came, Courtland Hightower, this is where you belong."

He took her to a nearby restaurant where they talked about philosophy and Negro preachers and W. E. B. Du Bois and the meaning of freedom.

"Nothing I read in my textbooks makes any sense anymore," Macon said, wolfing down a forkful of french fries.

She was intense, her movements quick and edgy yet graceful. "I mean, we were debating the existence of God in a philosophy class last week and I wondered what difference it makes what the answer is in a world where everybody says God is on their side."

"God's not the question or the answer," Courtland said.

"Don't you believe?" she asked, startled, surprised.

"Sure I do. In me. Don't give me that heaven pie in the sky crap."

"That's what saw our people through," she said, her voice full of the confidence that unnerved him in a woman so young and that made it impossible for him to move out of its reach.

"That's what *duped* our people."

"Nat Turner was a preacher."

"He believed in the avenging God of the Old Testament, not the forgiving Jesus of the New."

"You couldn't work in the movement if you didn't have faith," Macon said.

"Why not?"

"You don't strike me as a materialist, Courtland, there's more to you than that."

"Macon, I just don't believe you really buy into their God."

"I don't. I believe in my own."

"Your own, huh? So it's all relative," he laughed.

"Tell me something that isn't."

"Macon, what do you want from me?" Courtland asked, leaning closer to her, wearied, energized by her tenacity, the flamboyance of her spirit.

"Everything," she told him, pushing her empty plate and half-filled cup aside.

"Do you even know what *everything* means?"

37

"You'll tell me."

Courtland looked at the girl. He had done his homework, had found out through friends in the city that Macon was a hard worker, outspoken, tough.

"And yes, I'm a virgin," she said, breaking into his thoughts. "You won't hold that against me, will you?"

"You're too much," Courtland concluded, his heart pounding, excited and tense. "Girl, you scare me," he said, feeling his tongue grow heavy, fearing he'd soon begin to stammer.

"I can't take anything you don't give."

"How old *are* you?" he asked in exasperation.

"I've been here before," she said seriously. "I believe in God and reincarnation."

"You would."

"Will you believe in me?" Macon asked gently. "At least give it a try?"

"Sure, sure," Courtland told her, motioning for the waitress, eager to leave, suddenly terrified of the attraction he felt for this girl who was so direct, obtuse and utterly original.

In front of her dorm, Courtland told her, "Listen, I've got no time for what I think you want."

"You won't know that until you stop resisting me."

The warm April evening hovered around them, a quarter moon appearing to be precariously lodged in the sky. He wanted to hold her yet was more afraid what such an action would do to him than say to her. As she had done more than once that evening, Macon read his mind and wrapped her arms around his waist, her head against his chest.

"It's been a long time, Macon, a real long time," he whispered into the night.

"They say it's like swimming. You never forget. If you need to know how, it comes back."

"They're not always right."

"If you want them to be," she said hopefully.

"Give me time. Don't write for a while," he pleaded.

"I have to. Those letters to you are the only thing that makes sense anymore. They're the only thing that's real."

"I can't promise to answer."

"I don't need an answer," she said, gazing up at him, her eyes tiny silver pools in the darkness. "I just need you here."

Soon he was visiting her every few weeks, bringing her books to read. Macon wrote him often, but he didn't answer the letters, instead he just showed up at her dorm. Courtland was afraid to make love to her, because she had this crazy kind of hold on him. Every time he promised himself he wasn't going back to Greensboro because he didn't have time, he headed to see her again. Finally, Macon seduced him in the backseat of a friend's car that he had driven from Memphis to see her.

After they had sex she didn't make him feel like a possession, as if he were indebted to her forever because of what they had done. Macon made him feel as though she had to have him but could nonetheless live without him. Courtland had prepared no weapons to defeat such a sophisticated, measured manifestation of love.

Love mugged him, he'd later tell friends, and when it demanded everything he had, he opened his pockets and emptied them.

WHEN SHE GRADUATED from Bennett and married Courtland, they went to live in Greenwood, staying with his mother for the first several months. Ursiline Hightower was a tall, imposing woman whose Indian blood found expression in her prominent cheekbones and mass of thick straight hair. She was a midwife who had suffered six miscarriages before finally giving birth to Courtland. Macon sometimes drove with Ursiline Hightower to deliver babies, in her 1945 Pontiac, a vehicular relic that nonetheless traveled the roads of the Delta with considerable assurance. Macon assisted Ursiline at the births that took place on mattresses on the floor, on porches, in one-room houses where a dozen children played noisily outside the curtainless windows or slept on the floor around their feet. Nothing in Macon's Richmond, Virginia, background prepared her for what she saw in Mississippi. Yet she felt that driving across the Delta with Courtland's mother, who had delivered at last count three hundred babies, had prepared her for everything she'd done since.

The phone rang again, and Macon, as if fleeing from the sound, moved closer to Courtland. She wouldn't answer it this time. She would take a chance. When the phone stopped, Macon thought of their children—where would they be born? But she had learned to take nothing for granted. Before bed that evening, alone in their room, Courtland and Macon had talked about the three missing civil rights workers—Goodman, Chaney and Schwerner—who had disappeared near Meridian. Courtland was convinced they were dead. Sitting on their bed in an undershirt and boxer shorts, wan and tired from his days in prison, Courtland shook his head and said, "God knows I wish I didn't feel it in my gut. But I was born down here. I know what can happen."

He was losing weight, Macon noticed, his cheeks nearly sunken. He reminded her of pictures she had seen of Gandhi, ascetic and obsessed yet unperturbed. But her husband was no prophet, no saint, she knew. And they had even managed to kill Gandhi. All the purity of heart and love in the world hadn't saved him.

"But with all the reporters and the TV cameras following these white kids around? How could they be so stupid?" Macon argued. "Even if what you say is true, they won't get away with it. They can't."

"There'll be a trial and a jury of their peers and they'll get off. Look at what happened with Medgar," Courtland said wearily.

The search for the three men involved dredging the rivers of the state. In the past few weeks a score of anonymous, long disappeared Negro bodies had been brought out of the terrible Mississippi waters. These missing people had sparked no nationwide or even local manhunt. They had been considered just another nigger gone by whites, by Negroes an issue that, if pursued, could result in other disappearances. But as more and more bodies were found in the black communities of the Delta, the day of reckoning arrived. Children's questioning eyes inspired overdue revelation, and long-dreaded encounters with a truth parents denied more to spare themselves than their offspring. Family members dreamed of and remembered transgressions that had put those who disappeared and were now found in jeopardy. The truth washed ashore along with the dead.

The movement was creating bonds between black and white that were tenacious and tenuous. Lying next to Courtland, she thought of the clandestine affair between their friends, Marlon Jeeter and Carolyn Seavers, who had proven to be one of the most hard-working people in the Freedom School. Marlon had confided in her about his affair with Carolyn, saying, "She's just so different, so special. I mean I never met anybody like her." He sat on the steps of the Freedom House next to Macon, jittery with infatuation and desire. "She's just so different," he kept saying, an amazed smile flickering across his face. Macon fought to control the bitterness she felt in the face of Marlon's admission, but lost the battle, saying angrily, "She's white, Marlon, that's all, she's white."

She had begun to pray fervently and often. She prayed in the rapturous midst of the Sunday sermon beside the Greenwood women fanning and sweating, and praying and testifying and amening. She prayed driving along the back roads she traveled, and as she escorted someone into the courthouse. She prayed when the sun came up and when it went down. And the prayer, a simple God be with me, convinced her that she and Courtland and their friends would somehow be all right.

IT WAS TWO o'clock in the afternoon, the extravagant sun and heat melting even the hardiest souls. Jessie was lying on her bed, resting up for the evening session at the Freedom School when Lincoln entered her room. He sat on the edge of her bed and whispered, "Jessie, Jessie, are you asleep?" She had been dreaming. She was lost and trying to find her way back home. Wandering down a circular dirt road that twisted mazelike and stubborn, a road that had no end. She had knocked on countless doors but no one ever greeted her whom she could recognize or who wanted to claim her. The tears shed in the dream had just begun to infiltrate her consciousness, were threatening to moisten her cheeks, when she heard Lincoln's voice. Jessie opened her eyes and saw his face. With a quick movement of her hands across her cheeks she dried her face. She sat up and Lincoln gently thrust a bouquet of black-eyed Susans between them. The plaintive yellow and black flowers grew in a small garden in the back of the Freedom House, along with tomatoes, greens and pole beans.

Jessie gazed in quiet gratitude at the flowers, whose scent was so enticing that it made her imagine that one day she would find her way back home. Lincoln kissed her, the kiss a complex language of entreaty, demand and desire. She had tried to ignore the feelings Lincoln inspired, feelings that she now felt nudging her out of sleep. Lincoln took her face in his hands and kissed her again and Jessie felt him in her arms limp with need for her.

Most of what she knew of love had been taught in her father's greedy, corrupt hold. So Jessie had in the weeks she had known Lincoln censored thoughts of herself in his embrace.

But Jessie had also learned the art of obedience in her father's arms, so when Lincoln kissed her hungrily, so hard, so deep that it hurt, she did not resist.

She liked the part where his hungry lips patrolled her face and neck, and when he pushed up the oversized tee shirt she was wearing and found her breasts. They lay on the bed, the heat the only thing covering their nakedness, while Lincoln gently held her hands, rubbing them along the masculine, slender curve of his frame. He said her name as if it were a sacrament, and let his fingers play in her hair, now short and nappy and free like Macon's. Lincoln told her how angry and hurt he was by all the things he saw everyday, and that she was the only one he felt he could talk to. On his way to Cleveland, Mississippi, the day before, he'd been shoved and hit by a highway patrolman who stopped him. As he lay huddled in her arms, curled at her breast, he said, "Jessie, you know, I wanted to kill him. I really did. I'm tired, but I feel like I got no right to be." And when Jessie told him, "Lincoln, I don't know what to say," he said, "Don't say anything, Jessie, just listen, that's all. Sometimes, Jessie, it seems like you're the only one that's got the time anymore to do that for me. Seems like, Jessie, sometimes you're really all I've got."

When Lincoln took her, entering her slowly, carefully, because he did not know if this might be her first time, Jessie closed her eyes and the part of her that her daddy had got to first rose, walked across the room and watched Lincoln make love to what remained. Jessie feigned pleasure, her father had taught her how to do that too. When it was over, Lincoln fell asleep beside her and for that Jessie was grateful. At least he would not hear her cry.

Once she was her mother's favorite. The firstborn of Olive and Chester Foster, Jessie had reigned in her mother's heart like the fulfillment of a prayer. Even when Mae Ann and Willie and Junior followed, it was Jessie on whom Olive doted, buying her the occasional new dress while the other children made do with hand-me-downs from the family Olive Foster kept house for. Three years separated Jessie's birth and the arrival of the other children. In those years and the seven that followed, Olive Foster made Jessie a confidante, a friend, a rebuke to the weighty disappointment of her marriage.

But when Jessie was ten, her mother went into the hospital for surgery. Aunt Eva had told her simply, "Your mama's sick and she's got to have something took out of her body, so she can be well again." But when she returned home, Olive Foster, a woman who had spoken with angels in her waking moments, seen God in her sleep and who had once longed to preach, was never healthy again.

She had had plans to study at a Bible college in Knoxville when she met Chester Foster, a friend of her brother's who stayed at their house during Olive's eighteenth summer. Chester Foster haunted her imagination like some exotic dangerous flower, the likes of which she had never before seen. When she walked demurely through the living room on her way to teach Sunday School, Olive prayed for forgiveness for the beating of her heart at the sight of Chester Foster's thick muscled legs poking out from under the sheet covering him on the floor. Chester Foster smoked cigars and had a gold tooth that winked at Olive every time he smiled. He had met her brother Lonnie

in the Navy, where they had both been cooks, during World
War II. Chester Foster shot dice, huddled beneath the street
lamps outside their house, and called Olive "baby." And when
he was ready, he plucked Olive as easily as reaching for an
apple on a tree.

That's what her mother had told Jessie, in the days when she
still talked to her about something other than the Lord. But in
the wake of her illness, she concluded, "God put your daddy in
my way as a test, to see what I loved more, the world or God,
and I let the Lord down." Olive's voice bristled with a strange
pride in the momentousness of her fall. When she discovered
she was pregnant, Olive told her parents and Chester Foster
married her as easily as he had taken up residence in their
home.

Within months of their marriage Olive began hearing rumors
about Chester and other women. She had let the Lord down
once. She decided she would not do that again. No matter what,
she would remain his wife.

In time, the children became a barrier between them. The
love her husband had declared irrelevant she lavished on her
children. Then a massive tumor, which she took as a sign from
God, was found. Olive took increasingly to her bed and to the
Bible. By the time Jessie was twelve, most evenings her mother
entered the house, weary and drained from the demands of
someone else's home, and went straight to her room, leaving
the younger children and the house to Jessie. She spent her
extra money on medicines, visits to doctors, traveling to see
root women. She bought herbs, and curious prescriptions came
through the mail. In time, her children assumed the unkempt,
suspicious demeanor of orphans.

Her parents no longer slept together. Stacks of *Watchtower*
and *Daily Word* were stationed on the bed stand in her
mother's room. And Jessie became the mistress of the house.

"You ain't my mama, so don't be telling me what to do," Junior scolded her brazenly when she attempted to enforce orders given by her parents.

"You think you special cause she put you in charge, but I ain't gonna eat no more of this slop," Mae Ann, willful and cocksure at nine, shouted one night, pushing her bowl of greens and yams onto the floor.

With Jessie in charge, the children bickered and raged, their anguish a brushfire consuming them. Jealousy, despair rained, like a storm of dry ashes, clinging to their skin.

And her mother's door remained closed to Jessie, who at the end of each day, her spirit mauled into a tiny quivering thing, stood before the door and wished it open. But the lock never turned. Soon she was gripped by headaches, bouts of fatigue, fainting spells.

Beneath the thin covers at night she could feel anger slicing her insides into pieces, chewing her up, swallowing her whole. When she woke up in the mornings, she held her breath as her hands rediscovered her body, trying to see if she was still there. Her father stepped in, however, and offered her a facsimile of what she had lost. He pressed spare change into Jessie's hand to show how he appreciated the work she did in the house. Sometimes when he got home late at night, he'd come in the room Jessie shared with Mae Ann and check on her, his hands fondling her beneath the covers. Alone in the house with Jessie, he'd sit her on his lap and rub her against his groin. Once he kissed her on the mouth, letting his tongue slide through her lips. Jessie thought she would vomit. The hard steel-like thing rising between her legs frightened her even more than the kiss. When she fought him he grabbed her by the shoulders and said, "You my baby, Jessie. I can kiss you if I wants to. There's nothin' wrong with that." She believed him. He was her father. He loved her. Even the night he woke her up for the first time from sleep and hustled her into bed with him, he'd told her that. "I'm your daddy. I love you." Jessie, confused and frightened, was grateful that in the dark, in her father's bed, in his arms, he talked to her, touched her, held her. That part did feel like she thought love was supposed to.

Inside his daughter in the dark, Chester Foster felt as small, invisible and minuscule as she, releasing into her every hurt. All the memories lapping at his brain obliterated forgetfulness. The awfulness of the act made him unreal, and in those moments the feel of his daughter's small breasts against his skin, the terrified hushed song she sometimes sang to wisk herself from his grasp, froze his heart. All this terribleness made him forget sometimes Hector Beaumont, the one-eyed owner of the general store, who made him kneel before him, take his member in his mouth, beating Chester until he did it without resistance, the scent of tobacco, licorice, old cheese and sweat swirling around the back room where Hector Beaumont unzipped his pants and claimed Chester Foster for three years that lasted forever.

And women were just a blur, all one face to him, one body. He came to hate his wife because she had not broken the hold of memory, had not snapped the back of nightmare. In Olive's arms he was the little boy again, each time, vulnerable and afraid. But when he took his daughter he became Hector Beaumont, instilling fear, not feeling it. Mornings after, he woke sick, unsatisfied, wondering what he had done. Knowing all too well. If he could kill himself, he thought, it would be over. But he'd never do that. Some poison was in him. Now that he had started, it was impossible to stop. Mornings after, Jessie stumbled from bed, already in the hold of a skillful, perfect amnesia that erased the night from memory while burying it in her soul.

And so, theirs was a house where everyone had a secret. Mae Ann never said a word about Jessie returning to their room in

the dark, and slipping back under the sheets beside her, smell-
ing of their father's cigar, his whiskey clinging to her like a
second skin. She said nothing, but began to run away from
home so often that after a while, no one took notice anymore,
for they knew she would come back eventually.

Junior, the youngest boy, got into fights at school, and was
sent to a juvenile home for stealing sneakers from a department store downtown. Nobody in the family talked about Junior's behavior, or about the beatings his father inflicted with a
savage sense of mission. Willie took refuge in utter, complete
silence. He carved hundreds of tiny animals out of wood—mice,
dogs, squirrels. Jessie found them one day in a box beneath his
bed. He was so quiet they thought he was dumb. Chester Foster beat Junior because he was bad. He beat Willie because he
was afraid he wouldn't be a man.

When her father touched her, Jessie tunneled deep inside
herself. There she hovered quiet, unmolested, untouched.
Daydreams became the texture of her life. While cooking, she
learned to transport herself in her mind to a foreign country
they had studied in school, to sweep the floor and hear the
amusing, subtle laughter of imaginary friends. And there was
always Aunt Eva.

Jessie often stopped by Aunt Eva's beauty shop on her way
home from school or from the Bullocks'. She sat in the tiny
shop, surrounded by the scorching scent of straightening combs
and curlers, the acrid smell of shampoo and dye. The beauty
shop was a confessional. Here women flaunted secrets, told
raucous tales of lovers, recounted arguments with husbands
and employers, divulged their fears for their children. Jessie
swept the floor, gathering great balls of hair on the dustpan,
cleaned the sinks, washed the towels and listened to the
women unfold precious covert longings, draping them over the
dreary exterior of their lives. When Eva gave Jessie a ride

home, she noticed how Jessie was reluctant to move once they drove up to her house, asking Eva more than once, "How come I got to come back here? How come I can't go with you?" Concerned, Eva began visiting her sister's house when she wasn't expected and instantly sensed the chaos. She began taking Mae Ann and Jessie to her house for the weekends. When Chester Foster argued that they were needed to work in the house, Eva snapped at him, "Let them hardheaded boys of yours do some work, they got hands."

Her sister's marriage was the cause of her illness, Eva had concluded long ago. As she watched the two girls stuff a few things into a paper bag for the trip to her house, she wrestled with the impulse to go into her sister's room and drag her out of the bed.

Mae Ann and Jessie slept with Eva, watching movies till past midnight, drinking Dr. Pepper and eating barbecued potato chips. When Jessie asked her aunt why she never got married, Eva rolled her eyes and said, "What I need a man for? Just tell me that." And once while Mae Ann slept at the foot of the bed, Aunt Eva asked Jessie in the dark, "You got anything you want to tell me, Jess, anything at all?"

"Bout what?"

"Bout why you don't want to git outta my car when I take you home. Bout that no count daddy of yours. That's what about."

"No, ma'am, I ain't got nothing I want to tell," Jessie whispered, images of disaster filling her mind at the thought of putting into words actions she could never truly describe.

Eva turned on the lamp and gazed at her niece in disbelief that melted into understanding. Reaching for the girl's hands, she said, "You know, Jessie, your mama coulda been a Daddy Grace, a Billy Graham. But your daddy broke her heart and snatched out her tongue. A woman can unravel mysteries the average man ain't even heard of. Imagine that, Jessie, your mama living the life that was supposed to have been hers. Women don't birth babies for nothing. Man can't pull nothing outta his hat to beat that. And put a woman in touch with God, truly in touch, and you'll see a miracle before your eyes. But, Jessie, your mama looked at your daddy when she was eighteen and thought she was in love. I looked at him and saw a cracked mirror, a black cat and seven years' bad luck." Squeezing Jessie's hands tighter now, Eva said, "He snatched your mama's tongue and stole her voice, Jessie. You don't need to tell me a thing, chile, I can look at you and tell what he done took from you."

By the time these thoughts had unraveled, they lay like shards of glass strewn on the sheets between Jessie and Lincoln. When he turned over in his sleep, and whispered her name, Jessie scurried out of the bed, dressing quickly leaving him alone in the room, afraid to imagine what she would relive if he touched her again.

As MACON GAZED out the window of the pickup truck at the Sparks plantation, she saw the cotton field stretching before her for what seemed like miles. The field was placid, beneath the sun, content in the clear, afternoon sky. The bolls of cotton looked like flowers, resilient, staunch, clinging to the spidery vines.

"You know what you're made of when you work a full day doing that," Jessie said, nodding toward the field.

"Where'd you pick cotton?" Macon asked.

"My mama's daddy one time rented a acre or two and us kids would go there and help him out."

"But it's so beautiful," Macon wondered, turning back to the field.

"Yeah, from over here it's pretty all right. But you get up on it. Have to pick it with your fingers and let those burrs tear up your hands. *You* stoop over all day long, or pull a sack hitched to your shoulder, and see how beautiful you think cotton is by the time the sun goes down."

They had come to the Starks plantation to check on Glory Pickering, who had been attending the Freedom School and then suddenly stopped coming. Glory reminded Jessie so much of herself when she was a child that she had determined to try and get her to return to the school. During the drive, Macon had told Jessie, "You'll have to handle this, I'm just along for the ride." Jessie had begun to imitate Macon's walk, the confident stride she noticed most often in men. She had even let her hair go, just stopped worrying about it, cut it short, so she could look like Macon.

"What if her mama won't let her come back?" Jessie asked.

"There's nothing we can do about that."

Macon parked on the highway and the two women walked across the road to the plantation. It was noon and most of the field hands had taken a break for lunch. Jessie and Macon walked slowly through the fields. The Starks plantation covered seventy-five acres and two dozen families sharecropped on the land.

Jessie spotted Glory, eating a sandwich, sitting on a blanket with a woman and two boys. The girl was barefoot, her legs caked with dust. The plaid dress she wore was ripped at the shoulder.

"Miss Jessie, what you doin here?" Glory asked, amazed, scrambling up from the blanket.

"I came to see why you stopped coming to the Freedom School."

"She got work to do here; we need all the hands we kin git,"
the woman spoke up, pushing Glory back onto the ground.

"She was doing real good in her classes," Jessie said, looking
directly into the woman's eyes.

"Ah'm her mama," the woman said, moving forward, crossing
her arms at her chest, standing firm between Jessie and her
children. "She got to help put food in our mouths. Ah knew ah
shouldn't of let her come to them classes in the first place," the
woman worried, her dark face bunched up in fear. Sweat
rimmed the edges of the blue bandanna covering her head and
her life was etched in craggy stubborn lines across her face.
Two teeth were missing in the front of her mouth and the remaining teeth were dark and stained and appeared capable of
falling from her gums under the slightest pressure. Looking at
her, Jessie didn't know if Glory's mother was thirty-five or fifty.

"Did something happen? Did anybody threaten you?" Macon
asked.

"The boss man here come around to all us folks and say anybody what goes to try'n to vote or to that Freedom School is
gonna git throwed off the land."

"He can't do that. Not legally," Macon said. "If he does, we
could sue on your behalf. Sue the state through the Justice
Department."

"What that mean, sue? Sue gonna feed my chilrens? Give em
a place to live? Yall folks is trouble. Us gotta live here when yall
gone."

Glory's mother strode off to the fields, ordering the two boys
and Glory to follow her. Glory gazed sadly at Jessie, then
picked up her sack and trudged after her mother.

"I thought you knew how to pick cotton," Macon said.

"I do."

"Well, why don't you go on and let them know that."

"But what good's that gonna do?" Jessie asked, afraid to ap-
proach the woman again alone.

"Go on, Jessie," Macon said, "I'll wait over here."

Jessie took an empty sack from one of the boys in the field and began picking next to Glory's mother.

"You look like you know what you doin'," the woman grudgingly admitted, having failed in her attempts to ignore Jessie.

"I do."

"You from roun here?"

"Yes, ma'am."

"Well, then, you knows what ah mean. These folks ain't playin, they killin people over this silver rights business."

"I ain't been alive long, ma'am, but I seen enough to know they ain't gonna give us nothing without us pushing real hard to get it."

"She start sassing me since she been at that school," Mrs. Pickering said, fondling a palm full of cotton bolls as she spoke. "Askin a whole lot a questions bout things I cain't answer. Askin like she got a mind of her own. Come home and make me feel shamed. And even though ah made her stop comin to that school she ain't changed back to like she used to be. Ah'd always told her not to look no white people straight in the eye. And she'd listened too. Then she come home wanting to know why she couldn't look at em just like she look at me."

"I'm not asking you to do nothing that other folks haven't done, Mrs. Pickering, nothing I haven't done. Please let Glory come back."

"Ah respects what yall doin, but ah'm the boss of this family, and ah just cain't take no risk like that."

Macon watched Jessie from several rows over. She could tell she wasn't winning the woman over, yet Macon watched in amazement as Jessie turned away from Glory's mother and picked two more rows of cotton, filling her sack, before handing it to Mrs. Pickering and saying good-bye.

———

THE BLACK PEOPLE who walked into the Greenwood courthouse that summer to register to vote feared the required test as much as the phalanx of policemen and law enforcement officials who increasingly formed a protective flank in front of the building as picketing increased. The test consisted of a series of interpretative questions about the state constitution. The registrar, who administered the test, used his discretion in determining who passed. Negro Ph.D.'s had failed the test, legions of graduates of the voter registration schools had their tests marked invalid after a cursory ten- or twenty-second glance. Grown men returning for the fourth or fifth time and failing once again had sobbed like children in the hallways of the courthouse.

THEY'D BEEN MARCHING about an hour, careful to walk within the boundaries of the square, so as not to block pedestrians or cars. The protest, and the policemen stationed on the courthouse steps, had attracted a crowd that grew abusive and noisy the longer the picketing continued. A rotten tomato landed on Jessie's arm. She saw an egg fly through the air and hit the twelve-year-old boy in front of her on the ear. In the Freedom House, Jessie had listened to the arguments about nonviolence that went on into the early morning. She had also heard the workers discuss self-defense and how to mentally survive when under attack. But as the voices of the crowd— businessmen on their lunch break, their suit jackets flung over their arms; mothers with children clutching their hands; elderly women, their faces twisted in disgust at the sight before their eyes; young teenaged boys fondling baseball bats, resting their taut, eager-to-fight bodies on the fenders of their cars—

surged like a roar in her ears, Jessie simply wanted to run. A young white teenager threw a cherry bomb near the picketers. The explosion stunned and scattered them, and in the moments of confusion that followed, several young toughs waded into the group of picketers and began to beat them with rubber hoses and sticks. Jessie felt the metal sting of a hose nozzle against her cheek and instantly the warm flow of blood. Screams and shouts swirled around her and she saw young boys moving, running after the protesters, as though they were hunting rabbits. From the ground near a fire hydrant where she had scrambled, Jessie saw the police standing on the steps, silently watching the picketers being beaten. Macon had run onto the grass around the courthouse and lay crouched and huddled, her body protecting two young children who were marching with them. Finally policemen stormed down the wide marble courthouse steps and the youths scattered. The police used prods and clubs to round up the picketers and push them through the courthouse door to be booked on charges of disturbing the peace.

Eight women were crammed into a cell designed for two inmates. As they stretched out on the floor to sleep the first night, Jessie felt a warm trickle of blood between her legs. She had come on her period. She was so embarrassed she began to cry. Unable to convince the sheriff to give Jessie sanitary napkins, each woman tore off a strip of cloth from her clothing and wrapped toilet paper around it and gave it to Jessie to use. Breakfast was watery grits, stale corn bread and salmon. They passed the days planning even bolder actions they would take once they were released. Macon told them stories about Mrs. Ella Baker, who had been one of the founders of SNCC, about Diane Nash, who was willing to go to jail while pregnant and serve a two-year sentence for a movement-related charge in Jackson. Macon told them about meeting Mrs. Fannie Lou Hamer and hearing her speak. They sat on the cell floor and made up songs about those women and sang spirituals with so much conviction that drunks sleeping off a hangover, men arrested for vagrancy or petty crimes locked in other cells, added their voices.

REMEMBERING THE FATE of Alberta Garrison, Jessie swore not to be separated from the other women. Inside the cell the women created a universe that dissolved the bars that held them. All her life, Jessie had longed to hear people speak to one another in a way that made words an affirmation. Before her eyes, sisterhood, deep, spontaneous, blossomed into life. They fought off boredom and despair with confessions and revelation, each woman stitching a square onto the verbal quilt they wove all day and long into the night. Lovers, husbands, children, mothers, fathers, white women, white men, what they'd do when "freedom" came, dead babies, lost sons, hardheaded daughters, the books they would read if they could or if they had the time, miscarriages, their favorite psalm, sexual fantasies, the best-looking man in town, the most stuck-up woman, how they could never go back to *not* fighting segregation, dirty jokes, wondering when somebody'd cook dinner for *them,* wash *their* dirty drawers, how many days among them had been spent in jail. It all strode forth, from mouths censored at work, on good behavior, speechless from fatigue at home, strangely liberated inside this cell. And Jessie sat in the midst of the women, in jail, oddly content, daring now and then to toss a word or thought onto the burgeoning flame of their union.

Six days after the protest, Macon and Jessie sat in the cell alone. Over the past two days the other women had been bailed out one by one. Macon paced the cell, her energies compressed, screaming for release. Jessie sat on the top bunk, passive, calm, and said, "I never told you how I come to be here. I run away from home. Lincoln give me a lift and then I just followed him here, after he asked me to come that is. It's like in a way we was both running away. Lincoln wouldn't never admit to that, but that's what I think. After this," Jessie began halt-ingly, "I don't think I'll be afraid of nothing," allowing herself to believe this, hoping it was true.

"Every time I say that, Jessie, I get a surprise," Macon warned her, halting her march around the cell's circumference, slumping on the floor. "I hate this, I really do," Macon said. "I never get used to being behind bars. And why I'm here doesn't make it any easier."

"You know, I almost don't want to leave," Jessie laughed. "Being here with just us women. I felt safe. I'm kinda scared to go out in the world again, cause all my life it ain't been nothing but a man that's done me harm."

HE COULDN'T BEAR another death. So he began to write. Lin-coln sat shirtless in his room at the Freedom House, a small fan on the floor circulating a breath of humid Delta air, and typed another verse in a poem that was already three single-spaced pages long. The day before, the bodies of Andrew Good-man, Michael Schwerner and James Chaney had been found by the FBI. The civil rights workers were buried fifteen feet apart and twenty feet under the dam of a cattle pond on a farm south of Philadelphia, Mississippi. He couldn't bear another death. The week before, he had attended the funeral of Carter Lang-don, a prosperous farmer who'd been shot in the head as he got into his truck on Main Street, right in the center of town. Langdon, who had stockpiled over a dozen guns and rifles in his house to fight off the Klan and anyone else attempting to drive him from his fertile ten-acre farm, had just left the courthouse after attempting to register to vote. It had taken Lincoln nearly two months to convince Langdon to register.

"When I'm ready," he told Lincoln. "The day I do it, I want to go down there by myself. I don't need no escort. I don't want no protection the Lord can't provide."

At the funeral, at the Elks Club, Langdon's five sons spoke about their father. The oldest told those gathered, "My daddy was a peace-loving man in a hateful world. For all the guns he had, do anybody here recall him shooting anything more than a possum, less somebody aimed a bullet at him? Not everybody that owns a gun can use it. They was scared of my daddy cause a man with a gun's got something to protect."

He couldn't bear another death. The words had streamed from his subconscious, been released out of memory—all in a frenzy. Lincoln had sat down in front of his battered portable typewriter an hour after Jessie told him they found the bodies of Goodman, Schwerner and Chaney and had not stopped, eaten or slept since.

He was writing and so was healed. Scrambled between the lines rumbling into existence, transforming him and all they tried to render, was Jessie. Jessie, who had gone to jail and come out free. Jessie, who was in flight from something too awful to name. Her studied, awesome elusiveness bound him to her. If he had his way, she would become the mama he lost at three, the sister he never had, the family he longed to be a part of, the adopted father who died. He had told her everything, even as she hoarded her own past, sealed it against scrutiny. Her silence was a lock he couldn't open, with force or love. But it didn't matter who she was, he told himself then, or what she was running from. Now she was here. Now she was his.

And he had told her about being six and knowing God hated him, else why was love a torn, shredded hand-me-down, thrust at him now and then out of guilt or obligation, never just because. And he told her about being adopted and still feeling like he didn't know his name, about going one day to the bank with J. R. Sturgis and hearing him say yessir to the man behind the big desk, yessir, his hat in his hand, a wide nigger smile splitting his dignity in two, yessir and not holding J. R. Sturgis's hand when they left the bank because the man he knew had walked into that room but he was sure he had not come out. He even told her about the look Mrs. Sturgis reserved just for him, her eyes narrowed like darts that just missed his throat. And he'd told her how sorrow and sadness and grief made you free. Tasting them, there was nothing else to learn. You couldn't be surprised ever again.

Poems flowed inside him like the rivers Langston Hughes had known—the Congo, the Nile, the Euphrates. A play lurked in the corners too, one populated by his and Jessie's ghosts, by the corpses they had stumbled over to find each other. Bones would be reincarnated through speech. Ashes would turn suddenly into flesh. He couldn't bear another death. He would keep on writing until it was safe to stop.

SHE HAD PRAYED for those three men like she had once prayed her daddy would leave her alone. So, as she had feared all along, there really was no God.

———

59

THE PLAY DRAMATIZED the life of eighty-five-year-old Mattie Lee. In the one-character drama, Mattie Lee recounted her life as a sharecropper: the births and deaths of children, the two husbands she outlived. The play read, to Jessie, like a long poem, except the poetry sounded like Negroes this time. When she finished reading, Lincoln asked, "What do you think?"

"Why, Lincoln, I think it's the nicest thing I ever read. What you gonna do with it?"

"We're gonna put it on. Present it. I wrote this for you. I want you to play the part of Mattie Lee."

"I can't act," Jessie protested nervously.

"Sure you can."

"Oh no, Lincoln, no, I can't do that," she said, rising quickly from the bed. "I'd be afraid, standing in front of a whole bunch of people. I could never remember all those words."

"I'll help you. Direct you."

Holding up her hands in protest, Jessie insisted, "Lincoln, I can't, I just can't."

He walked over to Jessie and held her. "You said you were too scared to join the movement," Lincoln reminded her, moving in on Jessie and capturing her in his arms before she could back away.

"That's not the same thing as acting. Nobody's looking at me all the time, like when you're acting."

"You just think they're not. But they are. Look, read some of this out loud for me, won't you? I wrote it but I've never really heard how it sounds."

Jessie picked up the manuscript, scanning the paper, looking at the words as though for the first time. And then she began to read aloud, slowly, clearly, her voice trembling now and then at the knowledge of how assured and inevitable was the fusion of her voice and Lincoln's words. Eventually, she stood to act out the stage directions requiring Mattie Lee to kneel, lean over, lift imaginary bales of cotton and nurse a sick child.

AND DO REMEMBER ME

When she read the last line, Jessie handed the play back to Lincoln and said, "I like it Lincoln, I like it a lot, but there's some things in there that don't sound like things a woman would say. I know you're a good writer and you used your imagination and all but there's a few parts where it just don't sound real."

"Well, tell me, Jessie," Lincoln said, moving to sit beside her on the bed, trying to capture and hold her mood of cooperation, "tell me where it don't sound real."

ACTING WAS JUST like daydreaming, except you were living other people's dreams, Jessie thought. There were moments when she hated Lincoln during the tense, exultant days of preparation for the staging of the play. Beneath his demanding eye she read and then memorized the script. They had spent several days reworking some of the dialogue, making it sound "real." And when it all sounded right, Lincoln took Jessie by the hand and shepherded her inside the skin of Mattie Lee.

"Think about your mama, your grandmama, all the women you know," he'd urged her as she had moved from just reciting the words to living them. "Let them talk to you. Go back to your front porch, your backyard, the kitchen, wherever you can to track down these women."

And so Jessie approached it like a game. Mattie Lee became a skeleton she had to clothe, a phantom she had to find. But all roads, Jessie learned, led back to herself. Back to her memories, and her pain. Lincoln and Jessie fought and made up repeatedly as they gave birth and life to Mattie Lee. They spent eight- to ten-hour days in the basement where Freedom School classes had been held, locked, Jessie sometimes felt, in a prison made of words. Once in exasperation, she screamed, "Being in jail was better than this," and threw the script at Lincoln. If Jessie told Lincoln she couldn't create an emotion or a certain feeling for the old woman, he refused to accept her excuse. When Mattie Lee had to cry, Lincoln shouted at Jessie, reducing her to tears within seconds, then swooped her up in his arms, propped her into position and coaxed Mattie Lee's words out of her. When Mattie Lee had to get mad, he taunted Jessie, wondered out loud if she was as good as he'd thought she was. And, as Jessie charged across the room to pummel him with her fists, Lincoln freeze-framed her actions, shouting, "Now, Jessie, now, let Mattie Lee use your anger."

Jessie fell into bed at night, drained, her sleep vacant and deep.

When she made her debut, on the stage of George Washington Carver High School, after the curtain went up, it took her ten minutes to move her feet onto the stage. The makeup Lincoln had applied and the wig she wore, all to make her appear to be eighty-five years old, felt like glue enveloping her head. So blinded was Jessie by the stage lights that she couldn't even see the audience. Her voice veered between inaudible whispers and shouts that echoed up to the balcony of the auditorium, which was filled to capacity. Yet in the seventy-five minutes of the play Jessie risked everything. No one had ever asked her to surrender this much. No one had ever lavished her with such faith. When she stood on the stage, basking in the heartfelt applause of her Freedom School students, the women she had been jailed with, people from the Freedom House and townspeople, Jessie didn't know if she would ever forgive Lincoln for pushing her this far, or how she could ever thank him.

THE NORTHERN college students began to leave the south. Carolyn Seavers was one of the last to go. The morning of her departure, Macon and Jessie drove Carolyn to the airport in Jackson. Much of the mythology about white women that was once lodged in Jessie's imagination had been shattered in the few months of her acquaintance with Carolyn. Jessie had cleaned up after and born the withering scorn of white women all her life. She had seen the tattered seams, the sharp edges of their lives, played out in full dress before her as though she wasn't even there. Yet Jessie had imagined that despite the smudged, grubby reality she witnessed in the Bullock home, and in the home where her mother had worked, that white women's lives were nonetheless a fanciful, jealously guarded dream. For if their lives were indeed perfect, blemish free, if the world denied them nothing, then that would explain how ruthlessly those lives were guarded against intrusion by people who looked like her. Hardly anything she had learned this summer made sense. Hundreds of black people had been registered, but people had been killed, property had been destroyed and all her preconceived notions had capsized. Despite the litany of disclosures Carolyn had recited lying in bed next to Jessie, night after night, the girl remained a brutally complex equation Jessie was unable to solve.

From the backseat Jessie stole a quick glance at Carolyn riding in front beside Macon, and saw her staring out the window, her eyes on edge, tense. Experience, Jessie thought, looking back at the road. She now knew what Carolyn had meant by the word. She thought of the afternoon that she and Carolyn had walked past Lurlee Bascomb's tiny decrepit grocery store where Negroes could buy food, liquor and beer on credit. Lurlee had spotted Jessie and Carolyn out the window and had run from behind the counter, her cash register open, growling to the customers in line, "Yall wait here, I'll be right back," as she handily reached for the rifle that she kept stationed behind the cooler full of Coca-Cola and RC, and headed out the door. The grizzled old white woman stood in the middle of the sidewalk, raised her rifle with a hunter's skill and fired a bullet that spun several inches past Carolyn's head. "You nigger-loving, whore Communist," she screamed at them as in shock they turned to look back. Lurlee stood clutching the rifle barrel, shaking it in the air, stamping her feet, her thin sharp voice stinging the air with curses and anguished screams, threatening not to miss next time. Her fury spent, breathless and red-faced, satisfied by the sight of Carolyn and Jessie in flight, Lurlee Bascomb went back into the store and resumed selling food and liquor to her black customers. Meanwhile Carolyn and Jessie huddled in a nearby alley. Jessie was so frightened she had peed on herself, but Carolyn poked her head around the corner, stared at Lurlee Bascomb and raised her middle finger in the air. She turned back to Jessie and began laughing so hard that she couldn't stand up and fell on her knees in the alley. "That old bitch," Carolyn fumed, "she's crazy, and can't even shoot straight. Now if she was sane, we'd be in trouble." And she began laughing again.

Jessie recalled the evenings that Carolyn returned to the Freedom House, her arms and face sunburned from the long hours canvassing for voters. She listened to her awed stories of the homes she had been to that day, the people she had met, the poverty she had seen.

"I never knew this was America too," she'd told Jessie one evening. "I feel cheated because nobody ever told me."

"What would you have done if they had?" Jessie had asked.

"I hope I'd do what I'm doing now," Carolyn had said.

There had been long calls home the first two weeks. Collect calls to Minnesota filled with tears and threats, ultimatums and warnings. But in the end Carolyn had stayed.

Then there were the nights she crawled into bed late, having just left Marlon Jeeter's arms. So intoxicated was she with the sense of the momentous that on those nights she lay awake beside Jessie, unable to sleep, rousing Jessie to tell all the things Marlon did to her, the places he touched her, how she had never felt the way she felt now about anybody, how Marlon was the first man she had ever been with that way. Carolyn never suspected that Jessie would feel any proprietorship toward Marlon, that she could find Carolyn's infatuation offensive because of the sheer ease with which it altered history, circumvented white women on pedestals and black men swinging from the end of a rope.

But Jessie was too polite and tried too hard to like the girl to say any of this. On mornings after Carolyn had so casually divulged her secrets, Jessie could hardly look Marlon in the face.

"I'm gonna miss everybody, I really am," Carolyn said.

"Well, you can always come back. There'll still be plenty to do," Macon told her.

"What about you and Marlon?" Jessie asked.

"I don't know exactly what's gonna happen with us," Carolyn said quietly. "The only thing I do know is I'm pregnant." She said the word pregnant with the easy defiance that Jessie now knew so well.

"Does Marlon know?" Macon asked, alarmed, looking in the same glance at both Jessie and Carolyn.

"I don't want him to know," Carolyn told them as though issuing a command.

"Don't you think you owe him that?" Macon asked solemnly.

"I have to think about myself, but I told my mother and she's going to have it taken care of when I get home." Carolyn stared out the window, her face expressionless.

Jessie didn't know what Carolyn meant by "taken care of" but she was afraid to ask.

At the airport in Jackson, Macon and Jessie helped Carolyn

unload her bags from the trunk and walked with her to the entrance. Macon shook her hand and Jessie hugged her good-bye.

Half a mile from the airport, Jessie asked Macon what Carolyn had meant by her mama was gonna "take care of" her being pregnant?

"She's going to have an abortion. Her mother will pay some doctor to get rid of it," Macon said matter-of-factly.

In her senior year in high school a girl Jessie knew only slightly, Nadine Colby, had gotten pregnant. She was a buck-toothed, heavy-set girl. A story had been going around that a group of boys had made a bet as to who could be the first to have sex with her. A shy, lonely girl so self-conscious that she stuttered and sat alone in the cafeteria, Nadine had been re-markably easy to seduce.

According to the whispers that streamed between the stalls in the girls' bathroom, exchanged in front of lockers, when Nadine found out she was pregnant she went to some man who stuck a tube inside her to suck the baby out. Everything seemed fine, then the next day she started bleeding and didn't stop until she died.

"You think Marlon'll ever see her again?" she asked Macon.

"I don't know, Jessie, we're cooking up a strange brew," Macon said wearily. "This is what integration, brotherhood, means, and it's coming one way or another whether we're ready for it or not."

"But how can she just get rid of his baby like that? She spent all summer telling me she was in love."

"Maybe she was, Jessie. Maybe she was. But her parents have got her life planned for her. And they sure as hell didn't plan on nothing like this. Love or no love, Marlon is a Negro, she's white. That don't go down easy north or south."

"So then, when she gets rid of the baby things'll be like be-fore?" Jessie asked.

"It's about choices, Jessie. That's all it's about. Some people have them, some people don't."

Whenever she was late coming on her period and feared she was carrying her father's child, Jessie always knew what she would do. She didn't know how to swim so she imagined jumping into the Mississippi River and drowning, the dark muddy waters lapping around her, sucking her down, filling her lungs, which didn't have to stifle screams anymore, filling her eyes, which would never again have to see his face. In the days waiting for her period to come she wondered if she could slit her own throat or wrists. Death, she knew, would be the one time she could be in control.

Suddenly her life stretched before her, outside the perimeters of her father's grasp. He couldn't touch her and so, she was sure he couldn't hurt her anymore. She was excited and afraid when she thought about what she would do, where she would go now. Lincoln had been working on a proposal to start a theater company in Atlanta, a company dedicated to dramas about black people. And if he did this, she would be a part of it. Nothing had fulfilled her like the time she'd stood on the stage of George Washington Carver High School. All her life she had wanted to be somebody else. And now she could be, anytime she wanted.

ALL HER SENSES were prickly with perception, as keen as radar. Standing downstage, Jessie heard the voices of the other actors. With great effort, she held at bay her own lines, straining against confinement, waiting for release. She could smell the scent of tobacco ground into the clothes of the man sitting five seats from the aisle in the second row; she could hear a soft

murmur in the back of the theater; a crackle of lightning her-
alding a thunderstorm echoed in her ears. And though she had
not seen her, she knew Mae Ann was somewhere out there in
the audience. She could feel her, and she knew Mae Ann had
done as she had asked. She had sent her a ticket to the play
and enough money to take the bus to Carol.

Jessie knew the three other actors on the stage as well as she
knew herself. There was Carmen, who would change a word
here, a movement there, with each performance to keep, as she
told Jessie, "from losing my mind." Ernest, whose overheated,
bombastic acting style, Lincoln had not yet managed to tame,
would threaten to obliterate her in the next scene. She stood
marshaling the reserves she hoarded to go toe to toe with Ernest each time they performed together. Keesha as usual was
playing to the audience, stroking them, offering herself like a
prize, breaking the symmetry between the four actors, the
psychic unison this particular scene required.

Jessie stood full of all this, bursting and satisfied, edgy and
content, heading with each imagined word toward the play's
climax, yet praying it would never end. On stage she had no
history, no memory, no past. She was an invention conjured out
of singular words strung together like pearls. If there was any
feeling she would die fighting for, she would always claim it
was this.

THE COMPANY of the Renaissance South Theater had performed, as they often did, in a school auditorium, using the
bathrooms as dressing rooms. Jessie had changed into street
clothes and removed her makeup. Hurrying out of the bath-

room to go find her sister, she saw Mae Ann standing in a corner of the hallway. They had not seen one another since Jessie left home and they ran to embrace, Jessie hugging Mae Ann so tightly that she wriggled in her hold, saying, "Jess. I ain't goin nowhere, I'm here." Laughing, Jessie released her.

"You was real good up there. Real good," Mae Ann said, smiling in pride at her sister.

Jessie let her eyes roam over her sister's face. The broad, flat nose had earned her the nickname Pug. Her skin had cleared up, Jessie noticed, the acne that had scarred her face so mercilessly was gone. And she was taller now too. As Jessie held Mae Ann's shoulders and looked at her body she saw that Mae Ann was pregnant.

"Oh, Mae Ann, why didn't you tell me?" Jessie asked, hugging her.

"I didn't want yall to worry."

"*He* didn't?" Jessie began, her eyes widening in alarm.

"Naw. This here is Tyrone Marshall's baby. You member him?"

"Sure I do. You gonna get married?"

"Maybe us will, maybe us won't," Mae Ann said with a brusque yet playful hunch of her shoulders. Jessie had always yearned to possess her sister's spunk. Mae Ann had threatened Chester Foster with a switchblade she had found on the playground at school, the one time he tried to touch her.

"Come on, let's go down to the cafeteria and get a Coke," Jessie said.

They sat in the ugly green-tiled room, sipping their drinks and gossiping about Aunt Eva, Junior and Willie, when Mae Ann suddenly began to cry softly.

"What's wrong, Mae Ann? I thought you'd be glad to see me."

"I am, Jess, I am. It's just that you done growed up. You don't even look like you did before. You never wore no lipstick or mascara and you done cut all your hair off. How come you wanta look like a man?"

"Do I really look like a man, really, Mae Ann?" Jessie reared back and clapped her hands with delight.

"Well, no, but you know what I mean. Negro women been praying and paying for hair long as I can remember, then you go cut all yours off." She dabbed at her eyes with a Kleenex Jessie had given her. "You like what you doing?"

"Yes, Mae Ann, I really do. . . . How is Mama?"

"Why don't you ast her? I'm living with Tyrone and his folks. Daddy threw me out the house."

"They ever talk about me?"

"They know I gits letters from you. I told all what you was doing with them silver rights people and now all this. I don't think Mama is ever gonna forgive you for not writing her. She say she understand you runnin, she didn't understand you not writing or calling her. Said you act like it was her that hurt you."

"She hurt me almost as much as he did," Jessie said bitterly.

"And *him*," Mae Ann grunted. "Near bout drinking hisself to death. Been having real bad headaches ever since you hit him with that frying pan."

"You know, all those people in that house, and I was always afraid, Mae Ann. Always afraid and lonely. I never had anybody to talk to," Jessie said quietly.

"We used to talk," Mae Ann said.

"But not about the things that mattered."

"How could we, Jess? How could we?" Mae Ann asked. She was silent for a moment. "He said you cain't come back. Daddy say he don't never want to see you again."

"It's not just his house. Mama's got a say."

"Say you tried to kill him and if you come back through them doors he gonna do the same to you." Mae Ann expelled the awful words in a fast furious stream.

How could he kill me again? Jessie wondered. *How could he kill me again?* She had convinced herself that since they were no longer under the same roof her father couldn't reach her. *How could he kill me again?*

Jessie felt extinguished, buried by a grief that flowed through her body like blood.

"You got away, Jess, you got away," Mae Ann said, frightened by the look that had suddenly bloomed on her sister's face. "What it matter what he say?" Mae Ann attempted an unsuccessful dismissive laugh.

"And you know what's funny?" Jessie said, her voice strained and hollow, "you were the one always running, Mae Ann, you, not me."

"Yeah, but I never run far. I run like a squirrel or a mouse, just a little ways from the hole, then come back. You run away to stay. You got freedom."

"But I don't have you and Aunt Eva no more," Jessie said, taking her sister's hand.

"You got a man though."

"And you got a baby coming."

"Hell, you think I'd have this baby if I could get rid of it? I tried everything I could think of to make it come out early. Nothing worked."

"If I can rustle up some money, I'll send you a present when the baby comes."

"Don't yall git paid for this?" Mae Ann asked indignantly.

"Yeah, but not much. Living expenses."

"Hell, you ain't got as much as I thought then."

Jessie saw Lincoln entering the cafeteria and waved to him. When he approached them, Jessie introduced Mae Ann. Lincoln was clearly delighted to meet her and shook her hand warmly. "We're going to get something to eat, why don't you come with us?" Lincoln asked Mae Ann as he hugged Jessie possessively.

71

"I got to head on back to Columbus. It ain't a real long bus ride but I only got about half a hour before it leaves."

Lincoln and Jessie drove her to the bus station and after they had hugged her, she said, "Jess, I wish I hadn't told you what he said. But I had to."

"Don't worry, Mae Ann, you did the right thing," she said, patting her sister's hand.

But the stricken look that had passed like a pall over Jessie's face in the wake of Mae Ann's words remained. Mae Ann felt so guilty and ashamed of her honesty that when she boarded the bus she couldn't bear to look at Lincoln and Jessie waving good-bye to her.

THEY WERE spending the night in a motel that had begun to rent rooms to Negroes, before heading back to Atlanta in the morning. In the air conditioned, tastefully decorated room with a color television and a radio, carpeting on the floor and more towels in the bathroom than Jessie thought anybody needed, she and Lincoln were arguing. It had started over dinner in the motel restaurant when he asked her, "So when do I get to meet the rest of your family?"

"What?" Jessie had asked, alarmed. "Why do you want to meet them?"

"Why not? I love you. They're your family. If I had a family, by this time, you'd have met them."

"Who says I've got a family? I've got a sister, two brothers, a mother and a father, that's not the same thing."

"Well, your sister seems real nice. What are the others like? You never talk about them," Lincoln persisted.

"They're just people and we all happen to be related. Nothing special."

"People aren't all alike, Jessie."

"Look, Lincoln, I really don't want to keep talking about this."

He had let it drop after that and left her alone to brood over the fried chicken and potato salad she left untouched on her plate. She picked at a piece of sweet potato pie and then pushed it aside, too.

But once he'd closed the door to their room the first thing he'd asked was, "What happened? What did she tell you?"

"Nothing happened. I hadn't seen Mae Ann in a long time. It was hard saying good-bye that's all."

"That's all?"

"Lincoln, I'm tired. I want to sleep," she begged.

And so he dropped it again but he couldn't get it out of his mind. He went downstairs to the motel bar knowing his presence would make the whites so uncomfortable they would get up and leave. He sat in the bar nursing a beer, wondering as he so often did who the woman was that he'd left behind in Room 312.

She was going to be amazing one day. He knew that now. He had watched Jessie pour a hunger for perfection into her acting that made him, as her director, sometimes unnecessary. They had shaped a creative marriage so tenacious that it had inspired a trilogy of plays, all written for Jessie. The reviews of her acting in newspapers from Atlanta to Memphis to Charleston hinted at stardom for her one day. He loved her and yet was humbled by her talent. Often too, he stood powerless before her heart locked like a vault against him.

Jessie had arranged a surprise birthday party for Lincoln at the theater several weeks earlier, and invited friends he had not seen in years. For his birthday she had taken the picture of

J. R. Sturgis he carried in his wallet and had it restored and framed.

She had become the critic of his work that he valued the most, sitting up long hours at night listening to his scripts, challenging the truth and authenticity of his characters' emotions. And Jessie had turned the three rooms they lived in above the theater in Atlanta into a home, by using flowers, plants, colorful cloth and political posters to give the rooms a jazzed-up interior beat.

She had mastered the motions of love. But Lincoln wanted more. He never felt her joined to him, solidly, completely, unless they were working on a scene or reading a script. He had heard her cry often after they made love, and he had grown so used to her protestations that nothing was wrong that he now willed himself into sleep instantly when they finished. There were times that she sat next to him or lay beside him scripting some truth in her head that she could not release, but he could feel. Until she opened up, everything between them was a lie.

ONE DAY SHE would tell him. One day when she knew he would never leave her, always love her, forever trust her, forgive her anything. But, until then, there was nothing she could say. More than once she'd thought she felt secure enough to risk it. At those moments she had seen total pure acceptance shining in his eyes. But then each time the voice inside, her private censor, sabotaged her peace of mind and spit into her internal ear, No not yet, what would he say, what would he do? How could he love a dirty thing like you?

"CONGRESSMAN Courtland Hightower," Lincoln said, raising his glass of wine, winking at Macon and Jessie across the table.

"Yeah, that has a nice ring to it," Courtland laughed. With only three thousand four hundred and fifty more votes it would've been my name."

"Well, to the Mississippi Freedom Democratic Party," Lincoln said, raising his glass higher, as his friends joined him in a toast to the South's political present and future. "So, all along yall just wanted to BE the system, not change it, right?" Lincoln chided Courtland with a swift significant glance at Macon.

"What's this yall bullshit? You were there too. And you know as well as I do black folks change everything we touch, leave our stamp, our rhythm, our squeal on anything we get our hands on. The next twenty years in the political life of America is gonna have white folks thinking they're in the middle of a bad dream, mark my words."

Jessie and Lincoln had driven back to Greenwood to see Courtland and Macon, who now rented a small three-bedroom house in a neighborhood that had been all white only a few years earlier. Macon was an administrator of the local Head Start program and worked with adult literacy programs in the state.

"And that quote in the papers where you called your white opponent a coward for not criticizing the Viet Nam War, that didn't help much either," Lincoln said, enjoying himself.

"The Mississippi Freedom Democratic Party spoke out against the war before King or any of the other high-profile page-one blacks. I said it then, I'd say it again," Courtland said.

"No, this time you'd accuse him of aiding a policy of genocide," Macon said.

"Right, this time I'd be more accurate," Courtland shot back, then quickly drained his wineglass.

"We travel around a lot with the theater," Jessie said, "and it's hard to see the changes. I mean I know there are black sheriffs and mayors. But people are still so poor."

"In some places poorer than before," Macon added.

"You blaming that on us?" Courtland asked, raising his eyebrows. "We don't control the economy, set fiscal policy. And what we've gained was worth everything we paid for it, and it's worth more than some folks are willing to admit."

"The some folks he's referring to is me," Macon said. "We argue about this a lot. I say they gave us the Voting Rights Act, Head Start and food stamps."

"Hell, that's not bad," Lincoln said.

"But it's not enough," Macon insisted.

"They didn't *give* us nothing," Courtland shouted. "Name a people who through nonviolent tactics, political pressure, appeals to the moral conscience of a nation, smart manipulation of the press and marching with only a small army of private citizens as foot soldiers accomplished as much?

"Maybe we don't own banks or things," Jessie said, "but I don't know any black people anymore who would ever say, like I used to hear folks in Columbus say all the time, that we had all the rights we deserved, that a black man could no more be mayor or sheriff than fly to the moon. We got rid of those chains on our brain. That's the main thing we did."

After dinner Jessie and Macon sat on the front porch together, listening to the crickets singing in the shadows of the flowering bushes.

"Lincoln's talking about moving to New York soon."

"That makes sense, if you two really want to get into theater. I'll miss you though," Macon said.

"We've been having a hard time raising money for the theater and Lincoln wants to spend more time writing."

"And you? What do you want, Jessie?" Macon asked, halting the rocking of her chair against the splintered porch, awaiting her answer.

"I want to act. As long as I can do that, I'm OK."

"Does it mean so much really?" Macon asked.

"It means more than anything. . . . How are you and Courtland doing?"

"Fine, fine," Macon said quickly, reflexively. "He's away a lot traveling. And I'm busy but I still miss him when he's gone."

"What's it like, being married?" Jessie asked. "With me and Lincoln, just living together feels permanent but I know it's not."

Macon had begun rocking again, her head resting against the back of the chair, her gaze thrust skyward, seeking something Jessie wondered if even she could name.

"It's oh, so, I don't know," Macon began. "I feel like we're starting over every day."

"Does it feel good?"

"Sometimes. But, oh, Jessie, when it feels bad, it feels worse than anything I ever knew." Macon shuddered, drawing Jessie's anxious gaze.

"There's just so much to Courtland," Jessie said.

"There's a lot to me too." Macon stopped rocking and leaned forward to Jessie, sitting on the top step. "Do you know Courtland has never once said to me, 'I'm sorry or I was wrong.'" Macon told Jessie this, suddenly warm with the anger she felt sometimes when she and Courtland argued and she longed in the aftermath for him to shape the truce that he always assumed she would design. "Never once."

"Maybe he just feels it but can't get it out. I'm like that sometimes myself," Jessie told her.

"You should've seen him during the campaign. Something happened to him standing before a crowd of people selling them his version of their dreams," Macon said. "He burned like a house on fire. I'd listen to him and look at him and recognize him but swear I didn't know him."

"But what's wrong with that?" Jessie asked.

"And after a rally when we were alone," Macon continued, almost as though talking to herself, "there was just this emptiness, a vacant place. Nothing he said or did to me alone or we did together seemed filled with the same urgency."

"Maybe he needs all the organizing, the meetings, the efforts to change things. Maybe it gives him something you don't," Jessie said softly. "He can still love you and need all the other things too, Macon."

"Can he, Jessie, can he really?" Macon's voice was brittle with a skepticism so harsh that it punctured Jessie's composure and led her to say simply, "Macon, I don't know. I just don't know."

They sat in silence for a while, the voices of their men inside at the dinner table dancing through the screen door, sometimes settling on the porch with them.

As Jessie thought more and more about the possibility of leaving the south she had become obsessed with the idea of telling someone her secret. There was no woman she admired more than Macon, whom she still found herself imitating, using Macon's tricks, her attitudes, her forceful manner and style in the shaping of a character and sometimes just when she was playing herself. They had remained in close touch. Macon wasn't just the person she *wanted* to tell, she was the only person she *could* tell.

"I want to tell you a secret," Jessie began, her voice at first too small and unobtrusive for Macon to even hear. There, she had said it. And, as she did, she heard the little voice, but she pushed it back, so far back it couldn't reach her. "Before I tell you though," she pushed on, "I want you to forgive me for knowing you all this time and never telling you before. Why I never told you had more to do with me than anything I didn't trust about you."

"What is it, Jessie?" Macon said, moving from the chair to sit next to Jessie on the top step.

The voice in her head was mad now, enraged that she had stifled it, dared to ignore it. And as it puffed itself up, gathered steam, Jessie said, "Just promise me that what I tell you stays between us. You can't even tell Courtland okay?"

"I promise." Macon squeezed Jessie's hand.

"Well," Jessie said, "it's something I thought I would just forget one day, but it seems like I can't do anything but remember."

BRIGHT
LIGHTS

$\mathcal{S}$HE WAS LOSING him. Even as her words filled the cavernous, suddenly lonely room, she was losing him and she didn't know how she could get him back. The reader sat at a desk before her, his eyes glued to the script speaking the other roles in the scene. Her favorite scene. The role she was born to play. The director stood beside the room's only window, arms folded across his chest, gazing at her with a studied indifference she could neither decipher nor defeat. Five minutes after her departure he might not remember her name, but inevitably he would recall every flustered line, each unsure move she had made. She had been called back for a second audition, had not slept the night before, had done little in the week since the previous audition except think about this moment. Prepare for it. Pray about it. Now it was here and she was losing it. With every word, each breath, each movement, she was losing the scene and their attention. Had there been a moment in the last ten minutes when she could have reclaimed it?

"Mama, you don't understand. It's all a matter of ideas, and God is just one idea I don't accept. It's not important. I am not going out and be immoral or commit crimes because I don't believe in God."

Ever since she first read the play she had wanted to be Beneatha, had felt she was *Beneatha. She would have been, could have been Beneatha too, if she hadn't been Jessie Foster first.*

"I don't even think about it. It's just that I get tired of Him getting all the credit for all the things the human race achieves through its own stubborn effort. There simply is no blasted God —there is only man and it is *he* who makes miracles!"

Why couldn't they see or hear Beneatha in her? She had allowed some of the girl's confidence to rub off on her—wanting to be a doctor and talking back to her mama. If they didn't give her the role, give her what she felt was hers, she'd have to give all that goodness back.

The reader was saying Mama's lines, the ones that claimed her daughter, retrieving her from independence and blasphemy. Her head rolled back as though slapped, her eyes filled with real, imagined tears, too proud to shed, and then she said, "In my mother's house there is still God."

"There are some ideas we ain't going to have in this house. Not long as I am at the head of this family," the reader said, his voice dull, detached.

"Yes, ma'am."

That slap had only made her stronger, that's what she liked about the girl. Nobody could turn her around. She had gotten Lincoln to work with her on the part, over and over, polishing this scene until he got so sick of it he refused to hear it again. Maybe she had worked on it too much, had wanted it too badly. Was that possible? Not after she had let this girl get under her skin, walk down the street beside her. No, please, Lord, don't tell me you can lose something just because you wanted it too much!

"Like a child," the reader was saying, and in response she said, "I see." She was trying not to see the director's fidgeting, his eyes moving again and again to his watch. His mildly curious gazes out the window at Broadway below them. She let her voice drop, get real quiet, hurt but not defeated, and said, "I also see that everybody thinks it's all right for Mama to be a tyrant. But all the tyranny in the world will never put a God in the heavens!"

"Thank you, Miss Moon, thank you very much," the director said, arch, false, hurrying her out with his glance, urging her to be quick about it, to gather up her things and get out so the next person could come in. She thought she would throw up, she wanted to, right there in the middle of the office, so weak was she with disappointment, fatigue and hurt. But she didn't, despite the upheaval in her stomach, the horrible air in the closet-sized room, the smoke from the director's cigarettes, and wondering how she would be able to walk down the four flights of stairs to the street when she wished at that moment to merely stand completely still—still so that she could decide who she would be now and how to stop hurting.

It took her half an hour to walk down the steps to the street, because she kept stopping to think about what she would tell Lincoln, what he would say. She stopped twice and just sat on the cement, dust-caked steps. "Miss Moon," he had said, "thank you very much." She was Pearl Moon now. Pearl Moon. It was a name that came to her one night in a dream shortly after they moved to New York. In the dream, she was alone in a small boat rowing toward a horizon that slipped farther and farther away the closer she came to it. She stopped rowing and looked up at the sky and saw the moon glazed with stardust that filtered, sparkling, onto the surface of the water. She started rowing again, and rowed to a point just beneath the moon's embrace. In the vortex of that luminous, breathless light she felt herself touched by the hand of what she decided to call God.

Nobody would name a child Pearl Moon. A made-up name, a

theatrical name, a name too beautiful for a real person. And that's why she chose it. Because she wanted her life to be filled with ecstatic moments of grace like the one that had come to her in the dream. Pearl Moon. That was the name on the head shots she'd had made, and the postcard résumés that she figured were in the desk or trash can of every casting agent in Manhattan. Pearl Moon.

When she opened the door and walked onto Broadway, Pearl felt the city's tangible, overwhelming and irresistible presence momentarily snatch her breath. She passed the theaters, their marquees blazing as though neon-lit in the late afternoon July sun. When they had first arrived in New York she had spent whole days just walking around Times Square and the theater district, breathing in its promises, completely unaware of its efficient, perfected cruelty. The fast-food chains, the theaters, the adult bookstores catered to specific, essential appetites. Walking the streets of Times Square, Pearl had discovered her own appetites as well. The building she had just left was like many of the anonymous structures that loomed over Times Square. Sometimes it seemed as if she had been inside most of them; auditioning, trying out for a part, huddled in hallways with hundreds of others, hoping for a miracle in the form of a part. The auditions were terrible, endless periods of exposure unlike anything she had ever known.

In the year since their arrival, she and Lincoln had started virtually from scratch. Nobody cared that he had won a regional award for the trilogy of plays he had written for her, even fewer cared that the Renaissance South Theater had been written up in national magazines and papers. What had they done lately? What had they done in New York? Pearl was a member of the Negro Ensemble Company apprentice program, but she hadn't been on stage in a year, and she worked as a receptionist in a doctor's office to pay the rent. Lincoln taught writing at the New School and City College and had an informal but not yet lucrative arrangement with a theater company in Brooklyn to write for them.

She was nearing Lincoln Center. It was five o'clock and the streets were jammed with traffic, teeming with pedestrians. Gradually, unconsciously, she had abandoned the leisurely gait that had carried her across the terrain of her life in the south. Now Pearl walked, like everybody else in Manhattan, as though her life depended on it. She walked as though in flight from unimaginable, yet certainly impending, danger. She walked as though the essence of life itself lay in the speedy, efficient propulsion of her arms and legs. She walked now, she was sure, with more purpose than she had ever possessed before.

When Pearl opened the door of the Gingerman, she immediately saw Simone at a table near the front window. Simone was wearing a wig so Pearl figured she must have had an audition today, too. Six feet, pecan-colored, possessed of a laugh that could raise the dead, Simone—who only used one name—was pushing forty. She liked to say "pushing it out the way." A decade earlier, she had come to New York from Kansas City with plans to make it big, and had been only marginally successful, playing small, sporadic roles on a couple of the daytime soap operas, being an understudy for countless roles, doing regional theater. But despite her lack of major success she was determined to "stay in the fight" as she liked to say, because, she often told Pearl, "Honey, I got my pride, and I aim to take a bite out of the apple before it takes a bite outta me." Simone had started a support group for black actresses, which Pearl had found out about, and they had hit it off. The Shebas met informally once a month and the meetings were part therapy, part crying on shoulders and part sharing of information about what was coming up, developing in the business.

"Well, if you don't look like hell," Simone said, when Pearl slumped into the chair across from her. "Was it that bad?"

"Worse. I never had them. Not for one moment during the entire audition. I don't know what happened." Pearl kicked off her shoes under the table and rubbed one foot against the other.

"Maybe this wasn't your part."

"It *was*, Simone, I swear it was."

"Well, honey, you and every other black actor in this city or in a two-thousand-mile radius is saying the same thing this evening. A revival of *Raisin in the Sun*, you knew the competition would be crazy. And I warned you a callback don't mean you got the gig. You ain't got the part till you standing on stage opening night, and even then watch your back."

The waiter came to their table and Pearl ordered a glass of wine.

"Well, where are you coming from?"

"Told you I had that audition for the Coca-Cola commercial, right?"

"Yeah, how'd it go?"

"The director told me I didn't sound black enough. Can you dig that? I didn't sound black enough. When the bastard's back was turned I started rolling my eyes, makin em big and bug-eyed and mouthing 'Mammy.' Told *me* I didn't sound black enough. I was sixty seconds away from slapping him."

The waiter brought her wine and Pearl reached for it eagerly.

"I can see the headlines now," Pearl said. "Crazed black actress assaults director."

"Driven over the edge by stereotyped roles," Simone said.

"Were there a lot of people?"

"Now what do you think? If we'd had some fried chicken and some sangria we could've had a party."

"I just don't know what to do, Simone. I'm so starved for a role I'd do almost anything."

"I saw an ad for a role in a porn flick."

"You know what I mean. I feel like I'm just marking time until my next role. Nothing seems to matter unless it takes place under the lights, on stage."

"I was a stripper once, between jobs," Simone confessed, her eyes clouding at the memory. "But since I invested in those singing lessons I can usually rustle something up," she said brightly. "I tell you, Pearl, you could do worse than to oil them vocal cords, get out there and learn to sing and dance like all good darkies do."

"Simone, I worked so hard," Pearl pleaded.

"And, honey, tomorrow is another day. I'm not putting you or your old man down when I say this, but you had it easy, kid, down there in the south. What actress wouldn't give her right arm to be sleeping with the playwright and the director. The competition for parts in the Renaissance South troupe wasn't nothing compared to the competition you're facing now. Maybe you weren't coddled but you had it a lot easier than most actresses ever get it. I've seen you in the workshop productions, and I know you're *good,* Pearl. But, sister, this is the big time and the streets are crowded. There's hundreds of hungry brown babies out there and you're just one."

"I THINK WE can do it, man, I really think we can," Raj said, picking up Lincoln's manuscript, thumbing through it and then tossing it onto his desk. "It's powerful. With the grant we just finished doing the paperwork on we could mount it in a couple of months." The phone rang, and Raj boomed into the receiver, "Yeah I been waiting to hear from you. Where you been?" He settled back into his chair and propped his feet on his desk. Gaining Raj's attention for a moment, Lincoln pointed to the theater area and began easing out of the office quietly.

From Raj's office Lincoln walked onto the stage of the three-hundred-seat theater. It was ninety-eight degrees outside but the theater was as drafty as a barn. The seats faced Lincoln in various stages of disrepair, some with ripped covers, others soiled and stained. An odorous fog of plaster and paint hung over the theater from the constant need to patch and repair the building inside and out. Still it was a theater, and soon his play would unfold on its stage.

When he and Pearl arrived in New York the play possessed the same soft, rounded edges that had always characterized his work. But he had hooked up with Raj and taken the temperature of the city, talked to some other playwrights. Soon he could see and feel his work becoming bolder, edgier. Already he had notes for a more radical play, one set in a post-black-revolutionary America. Maybe the stage was the only place the revolution would happen. If that was the way it turned out he wanted to be one of the people who at least made it happen there.

Lincoln and Raj had hit it off immediately. Raj was familiar with his work, thought well of it, but, when they first met, he was between grants and had no money to bring on a resident playwright. So they just hung out together. Lincoln would stop by and they'd sit in Raj's office or go to a nearby bar for a drink and talk for hours.

Raj Ali was a gargantuan, bearded man whose face was as pliable and surprising as a mask. Moods flitted across his visage with a volatile, frightening speed. His jokes possessed the brusqueness of a threat and his praise hungered for entry into whatever secrets the recipient had not yet revealed. Raj had served time in prison but wouldn't talk about why, though Lincoln had heard rumors of a murder charge. While Lincoln was developing plays in the south, Raj was reading his poetry in bars, and writing over a dozen experimental/third-stream plays with themes that were rooted in African mythology and history, metaphysics and astrology, all of which he had studied in prison. With a band of supporters he had squatted in the building that now housed the theater company and Mau-Maued the borough president's office into turning it over to them to use for a community theater.

Raj eased his huge frame onto the edge of the stage beside Lincoln and sat down.

"We're gonna be hellified, Lincoln, you and me, just hellified," he promised. "You just got to get a little more angry, get mad, brother, mad as hell. Black rage is the thing," he laughed.

"Yeah, folks'll pay to hear it but they just won't listen," Lincoln agreed.

"So what? I consider myself a revolutionary but there's only so much plays can do, ask Mao or Fidel, they'll tell you where real power comes from. But right now, Lincoln, you got the chance to be a hero. Everywhere you look the heroes are the cultural folk. And whites financing it all. Lining up on Broadway to hear us tell them to kiss our ass, now can you dig that? Only in America, man, only in America. You got bloods performing African rituals on the stage in Harlem, shuffling and jiving and slapping palms on Forty-seventh Street, casting spells and traditional dramas down in the Village and raising political hell in Brooklyn. Man, I got out of jail just in time."

Yeah, only in America, Lincoln thought. He saw as many dashikis as three-piece suits. Every black person he knew who was in the system claimed he was only on the inside so he could change it.

Hustler, political idealogue, manipulator, call him what you like, and Lincoln had heard Raj called that and more, they sat at that moment on the stage of a theater that Raj controlled and was waiting for the city to loan him the money to renovate.

Raj had lent him books on African philosophy, history, metaphysics, as well as a copy of the Egyptian *Book of the Dead.* Lincoln often wondered if this intellectual and cultural exchange was Raj's way of justifying his own choices.

The woman a man chooses to love, how many women he needs to possess, was, Lincoln felt, as accurate a barometer of his politics as the vote he cast. Raj Ali was the father of five children. The husband to two wives. Though they were not Muslim, his wives, whenever Lincoln saw them, were veiled, and long clothes swathed their bodies. Their faces were cut in two by cloth, their eyes and forehead a stunning half-moon. Yet even beneath the veils the women were not extinguished. Their uniqueness had resisted suppression. Malika's reticent composure was elegant and staunch. She crossed the room like a Masai, her face possessing a fragile, Ethiopian beauty. Fundi's vitality turned her veil into a kind of regalia encasing but not diluting the aura of sexual intensity that hovered around her like a perfume. Prurient interest, and plain curiosity, had blazed inside Lincoln when he'd learned of Raj's polygamous marriage.

One afternoon he had gone to meet Raj at his house and the youngest wife, Malika, had answered the door. Though she immediately turned her head when Lincoln entered, he still saw the bruises beneath her eyes and the puffiness of her cheeks. He followed her into the living room. Moments later Raj entered the room and hurried Lincoln toward the door, saying casually over his shoulder, "I'll be back later this evening."

Outside in front of Raj's car, Lincoln asked, "What happened to Malika, man, what happened?" Raj turned on Lincoln, his eyes ramming into him. "What do you mean, man, what do you mean, what happened?" The militant denial that curled in Raj's voice, the combativeness of his stance as he stood gripping the car door, waiting for Lincoln to say more, doused Lincoln's nascent sense of outrage at what he suspected. In a moment of cowardice that he would always remember, he shrugged and merely mumbled, "Nothing, man, forget it." But the sight of Malika haunted him the rest of that evening.

BY THE TIME Pearl left the Ginger Man she was radiating the cozy reassuring glow that several glasses of wine shared with a friend produced. She and Simone walked to the Fifty-ninth Street subway and said good-bye in the station before heading off to catch different trains.

Later, walking along the sweltering summer streets of Harlem, Pearl fumbled in her bag and found a breath mint and popped it in her mouth. Lincoln had begun calling her a lush, making comments about the two or three glasses of wine she sometimes drank before bed, or when she came home from work, or when she was preparing for an audition. She couldn't bear the thought of a fight about that tonight. Not with everything else. So she decided to try two mints and prayed they worked. Sometimes, she now knew from experience, they didn't.

All the actors she'd met had something, some fix, some mantra, some charm, to get them through the bloody awfulness of their lives—the constant rejection, the requirement to sell themselves, to hustle, to always look great, to act as if they didn't need a job when they were really desperate for work.

Some were into yoga, others meditation; some did drugs, drank; there were Jesus freaks, actors who'd been in therapy for years trying to find out why they hadn't made it yet. She even knew some who used sex to ease the pain.

As she let herself into the lobby of their apartment building, she stopped to retrieve from the mailbox several bills, a magazine and two letters. Pearl opened Macon's letter and read it as she trudged up the three flights to their apartment. Macon wrote that she and Courtland were thinking of leaving Greenwood to move to Boston. Courtland had applied to Harvard's law school and she was sending out for catalogues to study sociology. She wondered in the letter how relevant school, college, would be again after all the years "in the real world." But she finished by saying that they both felt they had to get certain pieces of paper to do the things they wanted politically.

There was also a letter from her sister, Mae Ann. When she sat down at the kitchen table, Pearl noticed that the envelope of Mae Ann's letter was stained and wrinkled, the stamp pasted on upside down. The letter looked as though the journey to reach her had been as tortured as the feelings it evoked in Pearl. She propped it against the sugar bowl, trying to gather the courage to open it. She had fled home, family, kith and kin, changed her name, but looking at that letter she knew none of it mattered, that she would live and die Jessie Foster.

Before leaving Atlanta, Pearl had traveled back to Columbus to say good-bye to her sister. Mae Ann and Tyrone Marshall had married a year after their first child was born and now they had two other children. Tyrone was a trucker, hauling grocery items across the south for a major chain store. A quiet young man, Tyrone was as steady and as predictable, Mae Ann complained, as a tree. He made good money but was away much of the time.

When she entered Mae Ann's house that day, Jessie had found her brother Willie sitting on the sofa in the living room in a starched and pressed army uniform, sipping a beer. When he saw Jessie, he leaped from the sofa and hugged her saying, "My sistuh, the famous actress. Hey, yall, come, look who's here," he shouted to the back of the house. Mae Ann came out of the kitchen and hugged Jessie warmly.

"Well, I don't believe my eyes! What you doing here?"

"I had to come to see you before we left."

"Where yall off to this time?" Mae Ann asked expectantly.

"We're going to New York to live."

"Well, *scuuuuuuuse* me," Willie and Mae Ann sang in raucous, joyous unison as Jessie settled on the sofa, blushing, flushed by the warmth of their affection.

"God, Willie, it's been so long, too long," Jessie said, her eyes clutching the sight of her brother's gentle clean-shaven face, her senses overwhelmed by the scent of his starched uniform.

"Mae Ann told us everything you been doing," Willie beamed.

"The old man would croak if he saw you now," Junior said, entering the room noiselessly, his brittle glance rolling like marbles over Jessie. "On the way to New York City. Look like I shoulda run away too."

"You couldn't keep your ass outta jail long enough," Mae Ann snorted, "that's the only place you was running." A huge Afro ballooned around Junior's face, tapering into Edwardian sideburns. A toothpick hung limply from his lips.

"I'm going straight this time," Junior said. "I'm going to Jackson next week to get into a methadone program." He stood fingering the slender gold chain around his neck. His words were slick, unreliable, the promises dissolving as they were made.

"How long have you been out?" Jessie asked.

"Two weeks. Got out early."

"Just make sure you don't go back," Mae Ann scolded him as she headed back toward the kitchen.

Junior had been jailed so often for robbing stores, stealing cars, that Jessie couldn't recall his latest offense. But she did remember that Mae Ann had told her last year that Junior was now using drugs.

"You looking good," Junior concluded as though Jessie was an expensive new car or fashionable suit. "I'm going to finish my dinner, I'll be right back," he winked at Jessie.

"They shipping me out to Viet Nam," Willie said, reclaiming her attention, his arm thrown possessively around Jessie's shoulder.

"You know you don't have to go," she told him confidently.

"What you mean I don't have to go?"

"Lincoln and I know people who've left the country to avoid the draft. We know how you could get to Canada."

"That ain't me, Jessie, you know that ain't me," Willie said, shaking his head. Jessie wondered who Willie *was* now. In fleeing her father, she had lost Willie as well. He had been her favorite. She'd sat hour after hour on the back porch watching him carve his tiny animals, the effortless, easy affection between them offering Jessie a refuge she had rarely found in their house.

"Are you trying to prove you're a man?" she asked, recalling their father's brutal beating of Willie and Junior.

"Naw, it ain't nothing like that. I just got to do my duty."

"But it's a bad war. We've got no business over there."

"You ever heard of a good war?" Willie shot back.

"All I know is *this* war isn't worth your blood."

"Well, I'm going anyway. I go over there and I come back with plenty of benefits."

"You still carving and drawing?" she asked hopefully.

"I ain't got time for that no more," he said, pulling out a picture of his girlfriend, whom he told Jessie he planned to marry when he returned.

Gently placing the photo back in his wallet, Willie said, "So this acting stuff is for real?"

"It's for real."

"One day you'll be famous. That what you want, Jess?"

"She already famous," Mae Ann said, thundering into the room. "The only Foster to make something of herself."

They sat together in Mae Ann's tiny neat house and talked about everything except Chester and Olive Foster. Junior sat in their midst, jittery, wired, unable to sit still, as unknown to Jessie as a stranger. Because she couldn't bear to think about Willie's departure, she plied him with questions about high school friends. Later in the evening, Willie and Junior left together. On Mae Ann's front porch, Jessie hugged Willie tight and told him, "Come back, Willie, please, come back."

"MY, MY, MY," Mae Ann said, arranging her large frame in a chair across from Jessie. "If Chester Foster could see you now." They had settled in the kitchen after Willie and junior left. Mae Ann's fleshy, overweight body was concealed by a dingy robe, her hair was uneven and studded with lint.

"What's wrong, Mae Ann?" Jessie asked softly, longing as she asked this to retrieve some measure of Mae Ann's spunk, which their father had never been able to defeat, the crazed stubbornness that had set her hightailing it away from Davis Road, out of their father's grasp, rebuking their mother's silence. That fire had saved Mae Ann and now Jessie feared it was gone.

"What you mean?"

"You don't take care of yourself, you just let yourself go."

"What I'm gonna take care of myself for? My husband ain't never here."

"Willie says he's a good man."

"Willie married to him? Willie sleep in the bed with him?"

Mae Ann asked with a grunt and a shrug. "And when he is here, don't do nothing but sleep."

"What's really wrong?"

"Oh, I don't know Jess, sometimes I don't think this marriage business much agrees with me; motherhood don't much either."

"It can't be that bad."

"You been there?"

"No, but—"

"All right, then. I just feel like running away sometimes, you know like I used to do when we was kids."

"There was plenty to run from then. But you're a mother now, Mae Ann, a wife, that changes everything."

"Whole weeks go by when I feel dead, Jess, dead," Mae Ann whispered, her eyes bright, glistening and sad. "I'm yearning for something I can feel and imagine but can't name."

"You ever tell Tyrone?"

"You think he'd understand?"

"Well, what is it you want?"

"I don't know." Mae Ann fumbled in the pocket of her robe and brought out a pack of cigarettes. When she had lit a cigarette and emitted a stream of smoke over Jessie's head she said, her finger tracing the pattern of flowers in the plastic tablecloth as she spoke, "It's like I want my kids, sometimes I even want Tyrone, but at the same time I want to be free."

"To do what?"

"I don't know. Maybe nothing. Maybe something. Hell, I'd find out. Why I got to know this minute?" Mae Ann asked irritably.

"It just seems like all the married couples I know are heading for divorce these days," Jessie said wistfully, fingering the edge of a straw place mat on the table. "Remember when we were kids? Nobody got divorced."

"They couldn't afford to," Mae Ann laughed. "I remember asking Aunt Eva a couple of months ago if the men were better in the old days. She just laughed and said it didn't have nothing to do with the men. The secret to them marriages was the women. They just stuck it out."

"You and Tyrone might not have been made in heaven but you two give me hope. I hope yall can make it."

"Hope is a funny thing, Jess. We all got to make up our own supply, can't depend on nobody else's. You not going by the house, are you? You not gonna risk seein *him?*"

"I don't know."

"Too bad you can't even holler at Mama. She'd love to see you."

"How is she?"

"All right. She ain't working as much as she used to and is home a lot now. Daddy can't work much cause of them headaches you gave him and I think it's driving the two of them crazy to be alone together now that we's all grown."

"How's he?"

"You know, the same old bastard he always was."

"I'll write you when I get settled up there."

"You do that."

"I will."

"That friend of yours, Lincoln, he seems like a nice fella."

"He is, Mae Ann. He is."

"I could tell the time I met him he really loves you, Jess. That man loves you a lot."

"Mae Ann, sometimes he loves me more than I can stand."

THE NEXT morning Jessie left Mae Ann's, intending to head straight back to Atlanta, but she found herself driving to her parents' house instead. The street was now paved, and a veneer of progress had settled over the neighborhood. A few new houses had been built and the outhouses dismantled.

Jessie sat in the car and watched the house, wondering what she was waiting for, what or whom she hoped to see. She imagined her mother coming down the front stairs, her father walking up the street. Jessie sat, her hands clammy, wet with perspiration, the onslaught of a familiar fear making her head throb. Still, her fingers wandered now and then toward the door handle. Finally she turned around and headed toward the highway, speeding, risking a ticket, as though she had escaped for the second time in her life.

PEARL LOOKED again at the letter from Mae Ann and knew she would not open it. Not with what had happened earlier. She just couldn't risk it. Not today.

The apartment was sweltering so she turned on the fan, placed it in the window and kicked off her sandals. She went into the kitchen and opened the freezer in a vain attempt to cool off. From the street below the sounds of children playing filtered into the kitchen along with the sounds of an electric piano from somewhere in the building.

She walked the dark narrow hall to the bathroom and began to fill the claw-footed tub with cool water. As she undressed, Pearl gazed in the mirror and saw her face, still young yet strained and unquiet. She recalled standing beside the road outside Columbus waiting for life to come by and claim her. She hadn't had this face then. Could never have imagined, standing on that road, what her eyes, caramel-colored, clear and sharp, would see, could see that they had not already.

Pearl rubbed her hands across her cheeks as the sounds of a drum and a saxophone drifted into the apartment and whispered for the last time, "In my mother's house there is still God."

Lincoln arrived several hours later. The apartment had cooled off and Pearl lay on the bed, sleeping lightly. He lay beside her and kissed her gently, afraid, yet hoping, that he would wake her.

She opened her eyes and he kissed her again. He and Raj had eaten dinner at a Jamaican restaurant and then gone to Raj's place and smoked several joints. Now Lincoln was pumped full of longing for Pearl.

But before he could even say hello, she moved out of his embrace and said simply, "I didn't get the part."

"How do you know?"

"I know." She turned away from him as though ashamed.

"I'm sorry, baby," Lincoln said, reaching for her, trying to pull Pearl close to him to comfort her and to comfort himself. "You worked hard. Damned hard. Hell, *we* worked hard." He never knew what to say to her at moments like this. He, who had scripted a thousand moves and emotions for Pearl, could not script an adequate response to her pain. And so, bereft of words, he said nothing, merely turned off the lamp beside the bed and removed his clothes and lay beside her. The apartment was as cool as it would get and her body was damp with a light film of perspiration. He kissed her, his tongue deep, rummaging inside her mouth, sliding across her teeth. He could feel her sadness, her defeat. When he kissed her neck, softly, gently, Pearl hugged him tightly and sighed, the sigh wrenched from that place inside her that she never allowed him to touch. He pushed up her slip and his hands were full of her hips. He kissed her stomach and shifted her body beneath him, thinking how perfectly she fit. He was inside her and she was sobbing gently, the way she sometimes did when he loved her, as though his love was too much for her. A breathless moment of release seized her body and it made her cry louder but he knew he had not really touched her. Spent, Lincoln turned away from Pearl, for she had, as always, turned love into a performance in his arms. For that he would never forgive her.

They slept awhile and then Pearl woke, suddenly, perfectly, the way she often did, finding that she could not get back to sleep. She eased out of the bed, slipped on her robe and went into the kitchen. She poured herself a glass of wine and sat at the table listening to the sounds of the night—motorcycles roaring down Lenox Avenue, music from boom boxes on the front porches of houses on their street and an occasional police siren. Quiet, that was the only thing she missed from the south. Quiet. She could not say peace and quiet for she had never known peace, but she missed the quiet. For the deep, unremitting quiet, the heavy blanketing darkness of the rural south, had always made her think that peace would come next, although it never did.

She wondered why he stayed. Why, when Lincoln walked out the door in the morning, he came back in the evening. Why, when there were times she could not stand for him to touch her. Why, when she woke up in the mornings baptized by a rage so clear and dangerous she wondered why she had not yet committed murder. She slept alone at times like that, on a pallet on the floor or in another room, as though Lincoln's mere presence was an offense.

Once, in Atlanta, she had thought he would leave. There was an affair with a wealthy white woman who had sponsored a number of fund-raisers for the theater. She lived in Scarsdale and Lincoln began taking frequent trips to New York on business and then Pearl found out the trips were to see the woman. When she asked him about it, for she would not have thought to confront him, he told her, "At least she trusts me. She shares her feelings. She's not locked, sealed against me like you." His charge had begged her for a defense, but she had denied Lincoln even an argument in favor of their love. Pearl merely turned from him and his words, brushing them aside because they hurt too much and rang with a truth she was determined never to touch. Macon had assured her that it was probably a flirtation, a fascination on Lincoln's part, a seduction by the woman. The affair ended shortly after she told him she knew. It ended as though Lincoln had been merely waiting for her to discover that she could lose him.

They had survived that. She didn't know how, but they had. They had also survived the night when, in a rage, she looked at him and saw her father's face instead and came at him with a knife.

SHE WAS DRINKING. He knew it. Lincoln lay in the bed listening to Pearl in the kitchen. She was drinking again and there was nothing he could do. Nothing he could say. Once he thought he knew her. He thought this mostly because he loved her. Loved her intelligence, her fragility, loved the way she made him want to take care of her and how self-sufficient she was on the stage and how she honored his plays. He had thought once that he knew her. But he knew now he never would. Just after they arrived in New York, and shortly after she changed her name, she told him about her father. They had spent that day hunting for secondhand furniture in the dusty thrift shops along upper Broadway, and they lay on sleeping bags on the floor because their beds wouldn't come until the next day. And she told him. He lay beside her feeling as though something vital, necessary, had been ripped out of him, stunned, flushed all at once with a complete understanding of everything. And when he was able to fight off the feeling of dread and horror that had shrouded him like a veil, he asked, "Pearl, why didn't you tell me before? We've been together six years. Why did you wait all this time?"

"I didn't think you would want me if you knew. I didn't think you could love me," she whispered into his chest, holding him so tightly, her grip so strong, he could barely breathe.

And as much as the revelation arrived like some terribly belated gift, it changed everything. Now he knew why she was a phantom in his arms, why she often seemed to barricade herself against him. And, as Pearl had feared, the knowing was unbearable. At first he felt betrayed by the years of silence. Then he fell in love with her all over again, because she had borne what she had borne, because she could laugh, could make jokes, could offer affection despite all that. He was determined not just to love her, but to save her. To save her for himself. One day she would mend. He would be the cure.

He heard Pearl moving in the kitchen, putting the wine bottle back in the refrigerator. He saw the light go out and heard her return to the bed. He closed his eyes and turned on his side, pretending to sleep.

WHEN LINCOLN offered her a role in the play Raj was producing, Pearl rejected the idea. She was hungry for affirmation of her talent from another source, and longed to play roles different from the ones Lincoln created. An orphan, he wrote domes-

tic dramas whose characters fled from, rather than found, solace in the family circle. Misunderstandings, petty betrayals,
reconciliations that came too late marked the thematic tapes-
try Lincoln Sturgis had created. His men were strong-willed,
capable of raging with a kind of oblique grandeur, like the man
who had in the end become his father, J. R. Sturgis. His women
were elusive, flighty, seldom bound to home and hearth. Pearl
had played a hundred roles Lincoln had created. And now she
wanted to see if she could do something more, something different.

But sitting in the audience next to Lincoln on opening night,
she wished she had taken the role he offered, for the voice, the
tone, the core of the play he had written was richer and more
powerful than anything he had done before. Watching it unfold,
Pearl could hardly wait for the play that would follow this one.
The audience was rapt, silent with breathless waiting. There
were no listless coughs, no one shifting in seats, only an articulate union between audience and actors that Pearl wished fervently she was a part of.

During the reception afterward, in a large hall in the same
building as the theater, Pearl watched as members of the audience came up to shake Lincoln's hand, and theater friends con-
gratulated him on the play. Then Raj entered the room, pushing his way through the crowd, moving toward Lincoln like a
hurricane, and shaking his hand mightily in congratulations.

He always made her feel afraid. When she was around Raj,
Pearl felt as though she were strangling. He came to their
apartment sometimes and he and Lincoln would sit talking,
laughing, plotting their artistic strategy. The muscularity of
their movements, the intensity of their conversation, always
drove her from the room. Raj wore his maleness as starkly as a
confession, Pearl thought. She hated the condescending tone he
used when addressing her, the way his voice dropped a regis-

ter, the way he always seemed to be joking with her, never taking her seriously. She hated most the way he looked at her sometimes as though he knew everything about her. Pearl could almost feel herself shrink, disappear, when she was around him. She told Lincoln how Raj made her feel, but he convinced her that her instincts, this time, were wrong. She could sense the respect that he held for Raj, how he thought he was a genius, mostly, Pearl thought, because he wrote plays nobody could understand, but nobody wanted to admit to finding indecipherable.

Suddenly Pearl felt Raj beside her. It was always like that. She felt him before she saw him. He smiled down at her, familiar, too comfortable, too easy, and said, "You should be proud of your old man."

"I am."

"He's gonna go far. Are you ready for that?"

"I think that's really a question Lincoln should ask me."

"Yeah, maybe you're right about that. Maybe you're right."

He was dressed in splendid green and gold African robes and a fez capped his bushy Afro. He folded his arms across his chest and in that one movement made Pearl feel trapped.

"Lincoln tell you I'm thinking about putting together a company?"

"He mentioned it."

"Why don't you try out for it?"

"Maybe I will," Pearl said, hoping the lie would get him to leave.

Instead Raj's eyes swept her face with a surgical look. He laughed, saying quietly, "Don't shit me. I know you got no plans to audition for any company I put together. I know you don't like me. I just don't know why." He turned and left Pearl standing in the corner alone, headachy and tense. She joined Lincoln then, making a great show of kissing him and smiling in happiness, hoping Raj would see.

———

THE PLAY RECEIVED favorable reviews and ran for nearly three months. Lincoln got an agent and began work on his next play. Then in the spring, Pearl got her first stage role in a play being developed by a theater group in Rutgers, New Jersey. She was chosen for one of the three roles in the play after her third callback. She quit her receptionist job and threw herself into the rehearsals. The play opened and closed after four weeks, but her work had been seen by a director casting an Off-Off Broadway play who asked her to read for a supporting part and she got it.

THIS WAS LOVE. Forget about songs on the radio. Poems. Valentine cards. Scented letters scripted in a passionate, precise hand. *This* was love—the audience on its feet, arrayed before the actors like a roomful of flushed supplicants, so full, so satisfied. Pearl thought the applause would never stop. The audience was content just to stand and gaze upon *them,* the source of their surprise, the reason for the utter fulfillment that they feared would evaporate once they left the theater, once the lights went down, and the actors marched off the stage. So they clapped to honor the life that had surfaced on the stage, and filtered into the recesses of something they knew, suspected, denied, cherished, hid. To receive this homage, they stood with their hands clasped, like loving brothers and sisters, forgetting the dressing room fights, the on-stage competition. This sound would ring in her head for days. When a bill they couldn't pay came in the mail, or Lincoln asked again for what she could not give, Pearl would remember this sound, and this feeling. She would open the magic box and take a whiff. The muscles in her cheeks were sore from smiling, her fingers ached from holding Jason's bony hand, but she could stand here forever. Yes, *this* was love.

It was 5 a.m. and Lincoln and Pearl sat in the kitchen waiting for the sun to come up. They had stumbled into the apartment an hour earlier, from a party in Queens that was catching its second wind as they left. They had driven from Queens in the used Ford Lincoln had recently bought, sharing a joint of marijuana, stopping at McDonald's, eating their fries and burgers in the car. Now they sat across from each other at the kitchen table, tired, dazed, but too pumped up by contentment to sleep.

"You know, I don't think I've ever seen the sun come up, at least I don't remember if I have," Pearl said, sipping a cup of tea.

"You'd remember if you had."

"I wish we had a camera so you could take a picture of it," Pearl said.

"The sun comes up everyday, honey; if we don't get a picture of it now we can get a picture of it tomorrow."

"The sun comes up every day. I like that," Pearl said, smiling so easily that Lincoln could not bear the happiness he felt just looking at her.

"Pearl, you ever thought about getting married?" he asked, easing the words out gently, casting his eyes down at his hands, measuring the rhythm of his voice.

"Married?" she asked, as though she did not quite know what he meant.

"Yeah, you know, married. You ever think about us getting married?"

"Do you?" she asked.

"I have been lately."

She had been leaning toward him across the table, her hands touching his, her breath close and warm on his face, and then she pulled back, as though stung by his words.

"Well, why, Lincoln?"

"Why not?" he asked, growing queasy with distress.

"Why do we have to go and do that?"

"Why wouldn't you want to?" he pressed her.

Pearl shifted in her chair and looked out the window without answering. For a long time she watched the sun filling the sky, while Lincoln sat watching her, hating the way she made him feel powerless in this moment of truth, the way she reduced his desire to an afterthought. And when she turned back to him she said quietly, yet with certainty, "I wouldn't make a good wife, Lincoln. You deserve better. Better than me."

"You'll never forget, will you?"

"How can I?"

"I want to protect you, Pearl. I want to take care of you. I want you to be mine."

"Lincoln, it's too late for that. Too late. It was too late when you first met me."

"Then what has all this meant?"

"I don't know."

If he could have moved at that moment he would have slapped her. But he couldn't move, he felt too awful. He watched her walk to the window and stand there gazing out at the street. At last Lincoln found that he could move. He walked up behind her and said, "Just think about it, Pearl, think about it, that's all I ask."

"All right, Lincoln, I'll do that," she said, her voice as bright as the sun that had just come up, promising absolutely nothing.

When the play ended its run, after nearly ten months, Pearl didn't work again for almost a year. Then in quick succession she got a few roles as an extra for a television drama, and was offered an understudy role in the touring company of a prizewinning drama by a black playwright that had run on Broadway for two years. When the play hit Boston, she spent as much time as she could with Macon, who was working on her master's degree in sociology at Boston University.

"HE WANTS TO marry me. Can you believe that?" Pearl asked as they sat on the sofa in the living room of Macon and Courtland's South End apartment. There was a tentative, groping quality in Macon now that Pearl had sensed over the phone when she called to tell her that she had arrived and what hotel she was staying at. She had heard it in the eager breathlessness with which Macon had said over the phone, "Girl, I'm so glad you're here."

"I think you're the only one who can't believe he wants you," Macon said. "Of course he wants you."

"I just didn't expect it, that's all. Especially not after all this time."

"I gather you told him no," Macon said, questioning Pearl like a dissatisfied prosecutor grilling a witness for the defense.

"I didn't really tell him yes or no."

"Do you love him?"

"As much as I can, I do."

"As much as you can?"

"That's right. Probably the most important thing Lincoln's given me is a home. I remember him telling me that J. R. Sturgis, the man who adopted him, gave him a name, and how much that meant to him. Well, Lincoln gave me a home. A home where I could feel safe and wanted and that has meant everything to me."

"But, Pearl, you both made a home together. It wasn't just Lincoln. It wasn't just you. That's what he wants to hold on to. That's what he wants to make special. He's a good man, Pearl."

"I told him I can't belong to anybody."

"Oh, Pearl, how could you say that?"

"Because it's the truth," Pearl insisted, angrily clutching at this belief as if for dear life.

"It is if you want it to be. I've told you for a long time that you need to see someone."

"Yeah, and what you're talking about is for crazy I-got-the-time-and-the-money white folks."

"It's not. You don't know what you're talking about. It's for everybody, anybody."

"Not for black folks."

"Oh, so that's your excuse now? Pearl, you don't have to carry all this alone. You don't need to," Macon pleaded. "You're a black woman and so you think your back is a bridge. You're afraid tears are a form of treachery, admitting pain is a sin."

"Oh, come off it, Macon, don't psychoanalyze me."

"It's not just you. Me. In a sense every one of us. You hold on to that pain because you think it's your birthright, the only thing besides the contempt of the white world that really belongs to you."

"Stop, Macon."

"Why should I? From the moment you told me what happened to you, I had a vested interest in helping you get over, through, beyond it. Don't you understand, Pearl? I'm no analyst, I'm your friend."

"One day I almost did. I almost did," she said quietly. Pearl was sitting on a hassock beside an aquarium, her chin resting on her knees, her arms hugging her legs.

"I had a little money saved up from when I was in that play last year and I looked in the Yellow Pages, and called one up, even made an appointment, but I never went. I never went. The morning I was supposed to go, I woke up and knew I couldn't do it. Don't you see, Macon, it's not just telling them that it happened, they'll make me relive it. Relive him. Go back there."

"That's all they can do, Pearl."

"Well, I won't go," she shouted, "I won't go."

Macon suddenly possessed complete knowledge of the courage Pearl had mustered to open the Yellow Pages, to find the right listing, decide on a name, and then to dial the number, commit to a day and time, that in imagination would become as much a death sentence as a promise of freedom. And though there really were no words for what she felt, Macon said, "I understand," convinced that somehow she did.

They sat talking for a while about the tour, the cities Pearl had seen, the other actors in the play, about Boston and the people Macon and Courtland had met. They talked, luxuriating in the sound of their voices intertwined, purposeful. They prepared dinner together—just the two of them—since Courtland was out of town. Then while watching an old Bette Davis movie on television, Pearl asked, "What about children? Have you and Courtland thought about that?"

"Now's not the time to think about them; that's one thing we both agree on. But you know sometimes I wonder. I've never even had a pregnancy scare, not once. I wonder but I'm afraid to go to a doctor to have myself checked out."

"Why do you think the problem's with you? Why not Court-land?"

Macon shrugged in discontent. "A feeling, an instinct, a fear, I don't know. But I *do* know that sometimes I sit in my classes at the university and listen to the garbage these professors spew out about black folk and I could vomit." Macon made this pronouncement boldly, clearly relieved, Pearl could tell, to change the subject. "Nearly all the texts need to be rewritten, especially the ones they rely on for their version of our truth. I've had ferocious battles with theory professors. To put it mildly, I'm not too popular in the department." She smiled mischievously.

"Why don't you transfer?"

"And miss a good fight?" Macon asked with a laugh. "I couldn't sleep at night and Courtland would disown me if I threw in the towel."

SHE HAS NO idea, absolutely no idea, how good she is, Raj thought, as he sat near the back of the theater, watching Pearl on stage. She was playing a prostitute. A young educated girl forced onto the streets of a southern African nation by the ravages of war and the disruption of the life she had previously known. She was the strongest actress he had seen in years—elastic, assured. She held nothing back. Her body was serpentine in its agility and she could mimic anyone, brilliantly affecting perfect pitch accents.

She claimed and filled her space on the stage with gracious composure and when she was absent from the stage nobody could take her place. Yet she had turned him down flat when he had asked her again about trying out for his company, turned him down cold as though she could afford to say no to the possibility of steady work.

He wanted her more than ever because he now knew she was afraid of him. He could smell her fear. When he came to visit Lincoln, she hardly pretended anymore; she'd just leave the room as soon as he arrived. When he tried to find out from Lincoln what really made her tick, Lincoln was reticent, joking with him about the chameleon quality of great actresses, laughing him out of his curiosity. Sometimes he wondered if Lincoln knew the answers to the questions he asked so insistently about Pearl. He knew all wasn't well between them. He could sense the tension and sometimes it seemed as if Pearl was even afraid of Lincoln, of what he wanted, what he could give.

For all this, Raj was sure she didn't have a rebellious bone in her body. Not one. She was an easy mark. He could read people, had developed a kind of X-ray while doing time, and Pearl was an easy mark. It was like she wore a sign. He wondered who had put it there.

He wanted her. He just had to decide when. And she would be good. She would say yes, then, to anything he wanted. He had thought about what he would make her do, what he would do to her. She would be compliant, obedient. He would make sure of it. He knew the value of keeping a woman on a short leash.

Three weeks ago he had come home to find his wives in bed, making love, their veils on the floor, the children asleep and them wrapped inside the sheets on *his* bed. Walking up the stairs, he had heard their moans, muffled yet unmistakable, seeping beneath the closed bedroom door, dripping from the bedroom walls that he would never look at the same way again. And it was all he could do not to kill them. It was only Ismail, his oldest son—big, tough, strong—like him, who had managed to pull him off Malika, had pried his fingers from around her throat, while Fundi shouted at him, cursing and screaming, hitting him with books, pillows, the bed stand lamp. The neighbors had called the police and he'd been taken to the precinct and booked on charges of assault. By the time he made bail, he came home to find the women gone and his children with them. He could have called Malika's parents in Teaneck, Fundi's sister on Staten Island, but every time he thought of the two of them together he got so sick that he could not bear to think of hearing their voices.

Nothing that had happened had caught him by surprise. Not really. He had seen and envied how Fundi and Malika got along, how they communicated, always talking, sharing, as if they could read each other's minds. He had thought it was a woman thing, the way women were, nothing to threaten him as a man. For what men gave women was, in the end, what mattered most, he was sure. In fact he had been glad for them, glad they had each other. He was away at the theater so much, he had not had time in his life, on the streets, in prison, to learn the gentle things, the soft things, the woman things. Besides, they weren't for him to learn anyway. He had listened to their conversations trying to hear what they heard, feel what they felt, but had always come up empty. It was like that sometimes with the children, too; not the boys, really, for he was training them to be warriors, not to cry, to respect his word as law, not to lean on their mamas. But the girls were a different story; he felt as if he'd lost them already.

Fundi had been his first wife. A nurse in the intensive care unit at Kings County Hospital, she was married to a junkie when he met her, and she told Raj she wanted a strong man. Serious, steady, the oldest of nine children, who had worked and studied her way out of a Bronx tenement childhood, she was devout, patient, yet strong-willed. He considered her his rock, his staff. Much of the time her salary fed them all.

Malika, barely twenty when he met her, was a dropout from Sarah Lawrence who had brought him a play she had written, asking him to read it. She had attended a private all-girls prep school where she was one of only two blacks; the summer before she met Raj she had spent hitchhiking across the country with a boy whose father owned a third of all the real estate in Manhattan. But when she discovered she could write she changed her name from Eleanor to Malika.

She sat facing Raj across his desk the afternoon of their second meeting, her pale, near-white skin glowing like a translucent mask. She wore a nose ring, and huge, circular earrings dangled almost to her shoulders. She was dressed in a turtleneck sweater, blue jeans and a vest made from a blue and orange swirl of batik, with a matching swath of cloth wrapped around her head. Her green eyes blazed with curiosity, sparkled with the hint of permanent surprise.

The play was as good as anything he had read in the last year. Almost as good as some of the dramas in professional production. But, pushing the manuscript across his desk, he said, indifferently, "It's not bad. There're some weak spots in the second and third acts that I could help you with. And the conclusion falls flat. But for a first try, it's not bad at all."

"It's my third play, actually," she said, a tremor of defiance frosting her voice, and exciting him. "The second one I wrote was produced at school."

"You been in the belly of the beast a long time, sister," he said, folding his hands before him on the desk, implying by that act a judgment of which he knew she was aware. "And now you decided to come home."

"I didn't want to lose who I am," she told him shyly, as though admitting a folly for which she was not sure she could be forgiven, moving the green eyes that three generations of women on her mother's side had prized, and been married for, away from his face, to the manuscript in her lap. "That's why I left Sarah Lawrence. And when I discovered I could write, and what I wanted to say—"

"You came to the right place," he said, interrupting her, hurrying to quiet her, to yoke the onslaught of confessions that would inevitably follow. Looking at her he knew everything that was important. There was nothing more for her to say.

He rose from his desk and walked to the office door and locked it, the sound of the lock forcing her to turn and look at him. But the eyes, which he now saw shifted imperceptibly from dark to light green, held no fear, only expectation. And she sat still beneath his hands as he unraveled the galae around her head, letting it fall to the floor, bunching at their feet. She threw her head back and sighed gently when his hands rummaged through her auburn hair—long, thick—massaging her scalp. And her delicate, fine-boned fingers traveled up his arms, beneath the sleeves of his dashiki, when his palms cupped her breasts. He took her on the floor beside his desk, amazed at the blondish hairs between her legs, under her arms, and the pinkish ivory cast to her skin.

Malika didn't resist, convinced, as she told him later, that this act was the first of many that he would use to initiate her into an understanding of what she'd lost, had been denied in all the years before he discovered her.

Two weeks later he asked her, over Fundi's objections, to move in with them, to be his second wife. Her obstetrician father had written her off for dead when he found out she was pregnant by Raj and living in a polygamous arrangement.

The respect Raj felt for Fundi was balanced by the passion of his relationship with Malika. In time the initial jealousy the two women had felt toward each other had dissolved. They made no distinctions between the children, both women caring for and loving them all. He'd thought everything was perfect. Malika had grown restive lately, saying she wanted to go back to school, despite his desire for her to stay at home. Fundi had threatened to leave him if he hit Malika again. But these brushfires were nothing he couldn't handle, he'd thought. Nothing he couldn't put out. Now it was poisoned. All the time he'd thought it was *him* that they loved, when it was each other. He would never be able to imagine what they could have given each other that was strong enough to extinguish his hold on them. But he had to get some remnant, some part of it back. Every time he turned around, people were talking about women, about their rights, like *they* were all that was happening. The white chicks calling all men pigs, acting as if they just discovered they were oppressed and more and more of the black women trailing along after them, like lapdogs. A man couldn't hardly get no attention for the women grabbing it all: writing, complaining, picketing, protesting. And some of the black chicks writing shit about black men that was positively subversive. He had to train the next woman right. Show her who ran the show, who called the shots. Maybe he'd begin with someone who was smart enough to already fear him.

AFTER A DECADE in the theater Lincoln Sturgis was discovered. The second play of Lincoln's that Raj produced received equally favorable reviews and ran for four months before being moved to a larger theater off Broadway. It was nominated for an Obie Award for best drama and best supporting actor. Lincoln was profiled in the *Drama Review* and his agent began receiving calls for Lincoln to write movie scripts. Suddenly, anything was possible. Pearl watched Lincoln carefully, hesitantly, for signs of change that would alter what she felt for him. But Lincoln wore his success easily, as though merely relieved that the world had discovered what he always knew; he could tell a good story.

One evening while preparing dinner together Pearl asked Lincoln, "You're not the least bit scared by what's happening, are you?"

"Why should I be? This is what I've worked for, why should I run away from it now?" Lincoln stood at the sink washing a head of lettuce.

"I guess now the struggle is over," Pearl said, wondering aloud.

"Naw, honey, the struggle just begins. I just hope that for us things won't be such a struggle from now on."

Pearl knew that Lincoln was not talking about their persistent need to pinch pennies, to put off until tomorrow the purchases that they needed.

She could not bear the hope, the desire, framed on Lincoln's face, flickering like sparks at the edge of his words, so she turned from him and looked in the refrigerator, although there was nothing there that she needed.

"How's Raj taking all this?"

"He's warning me that I'll sell out if I set foot in L.A. He says Malcolm didn't die so I could write trash in Beverly Hills."

"Is that what you want?"

"What? To write trash in Beverly Hills?"

"Lincoln!"

"Pearl, I want to write, for the stage, for films, for whatever. And I want to earn what I'm worth."

"How much are you worth?"

Lincoln stood drying off the lettuce leaves in the spinner and said, "How do you put a price tag on imagination? How do you put a value on the magic you create on the stage?"

"But if you had to?"

"I'd choose a value that had six figures instead of five. I wish you'd go with me out to L.A. next week."

"How long will you be gone?"

"Four, five days. Come with me, Pearl."

"I'd only be in the way. Besides, I have some auditions next week and I'll be here when you come back," she said with a gentle smile. "I'll be right here, waiting for you."

THERE WERE no auditions, no tryouts for which she had to stay in New York. She stayed behind to see if he would return to her from L.A. The four or five days grew into a week and then two. He called her nearly every night, his voice cautious, excited, outlining proposals and story ideas he was discussing with producers.

SITTING IN THE apartment one evening, Pearl heard the buzzer, and immediately wondered if Lincoln had decided to surprise her and come back earlier than he said. He was not scheduled to return until the weekend, but she allowed herself to imagine that he might be in the vestibule, announcing his return over the intercom or saying he had lost his keys. She approached the intercom with hope and anticipation. "Who is it?"

"Raj."

"Raj?"

"Yeah, I brought Lincoln's typewriter back. We'd been using it down at the theater and don't need it anymore. I been promising to bring this thing by here for weeks."

"He's still in L.A."

"And I'm still standing outside your apartment with a five-hundred-pound IBM Selectric in my arms, bout to develop a hernia. Will you let me in? he shouted through the intercom.

She wanted to tell him that she was on her way out, or ask him to bring the typewriter back when Lincoln returned. But then how long could it take him to put the typewriter down and walk out the door? In the midst of these thoughts, Raj pressed the buzzer again.

"Come on, sister, let me in, this thing is *heavy*."

She buzzed him in, and heard Raj enter the downstairs hallway, his steps staggered and heavy. Pearl opened the door a crack and heard Raj's labored breathing, as he carried the typewriter up the stairs, stopping on the landing between the second and third floors to rest. The sound of his raspy wheezing seemed to fill the hallway, and floated ominously up to her door.

When he reached her apartment, Pearl stood behind the door, which was slightly ajar, and Raj stood in the hall, drenched in sweat, his face gleaming with perspiration, his arms filled with the typewriter. To Pearl he seemed to take up the entire hallway.

"Open the door, Pearl, unless you want me to croak right here?" He lumbered past her into the apartment. "Where do you want me to put this thing?"

"Over there in the corner on the floor will do fine for now," she told him, aware as she spoke of the trembling in her voice, the breathless, ragged sound to her speech, almost as though *she* had brought the typewriter up three flights of stairs. Raj thumped the machine onto the floor, took several deep breaths and plopped onto the couch, his bulky frame setting the springs off in a chorus of protest, his arms and legs sprawled in a blatant form of surrender. Pearl had not counted on this, that he would become, in an instant, an immovable object. She knew her eyes reflected the sudden distinct fear she felt. The door remained open and Pearl stood in front of it, her hands behind her back, gripping the doorknob.

Raj pulled a soiled handkerchief from his pocket and wiped his forehead.

"Thanks for bringing the typewriter, Raj," Pearl said, trying to control her voice, and instead, making it sound false, edgy and entirely unconvincing. "I know Lincoln will be glad to have it back."

"Sure, no sweat, no sweat," Raj said, then added, "I don't mean that literally." He laughed, his face erupting into a grin that seemed to devour the rest of his face. "Can I have a glass of ice water before I go?"

"Sure," Pearl said, releasing her grip on the front door and hurrying past Raj to the kitchen. As she got a glass out of the cupboard, Pearl tried to think of something to tell him to speed his departure.

Returning to the living room, the first thing Pearl noticed was that the front door was now closed. Raj relaxed on the sofa, his fez on the coffee table, his face awaiting her return with an easy proprietorial stare. When Pearl handed him the glass of water, she was careful not to allow their fingers to touch.

"Lincoln will be back in a day or two," she told him firmly, confidently, looking straight at Raj as she said the words, for they helped, she noticed, to calm her.

"Yeah, the brother didn't even call me once since he's been out there, not even once," Raj said, feigning hurt as he placed the glass on the table. "How're negotiations, as they say, going?" he asked.

"He's talking to a lot of people, discussing ideas but there's really nothing definite yet."

"Yeah, I can dig that. Babylon. I'm sure he'll have some stories to tell when he gets back. What you just standing there for, Pearl?" Raj asked. "Standing up like a guest in your own house."

"Well, I was on my way out when you came."

"Really?" he asked, his eyes hot with disbelief.

"Really," Pearl said defiantly.

She had hoped her attitude would encourage him to begin to leave. But Raj settled back even more comfortably on the sofa and asked her, "Why do you always want to leave the room when I come around? Why don't you like me? What did I ever do to you except try to be your friend? Even tried to give you a gig, but you turned me down, like you was Liz Taylor or somebody. Like you was in demand. Like you could afford to say no." His voice was spiraling, curling, slowly reeling into an anguished vortex of tightly controlled anger. Pearl moved to the bookcase on the other side of the room to reach for her handbag. From that vantage point, fear animating her with an unfamiliar courage, she miraculously heard herself say, "Raj, it would take me all day to tell you why I don't like you."

"Because I have two wives, perhaps," he said, standing up, the move propelling Pearl backward, quickly, reflexively. "Yeah, I'll bet that's what it is. But you don't look like no damn feminist to me. Not at all. Come and sit down over here next to me, Pearl. I can give you a lift to wherever you're going. I won't make you late."

"I already *am* late," she said, daring to look at him, feeling the apartment close in around her as she did.

"So you don't want to talk. What do you want to do, Pearl?" Raj asked, moving toward her. Pearl stood in front of the bookcase, fighting the fear that had rooted her to the spot. When he was two feet away from her she ran for the door. But he caught her, easily, grabbing her neatly, in his arms, lifting her off the floor, while she reached hungrily, uselessly, with arms and hands and fingers for the door.

"Please, Raj, please," she screamed, her voice frantic, belonging to someone else.

"Please, Raj, please," he mocked her. "Please what?" He threw her on the sofa and pinned her there with his hands. And when she looked at his face, Pearl thought in that moment, of Lincoln, wondered why he was not here. Knowing how alone she was, how helpless, strengthened her resistance. Yet she was impotent against him, her slender arms flailing, hitting air instead of him. Her screams came out hoarse, choking, the fear constricting her throat. Raj's hands had pushed her long madras skirt up to her waist and she felt the rough rub of African cloth against her thighs. She heard her panties tear and his fingers invading her, peeling her like fruit and then wordless and determined he was inside. Pearl surrendered, moving to the secret place inside her, crawling there, curling up, her hands against her ears, making herself small, so small, hoping she would disappear. Some part of her lived, always in the secret place, always there except when she was acting. Except when she was somebody else.

Even the secret place didn't help now, the smell of him, the smell of her, broke through. The walls were not holding. She prayed for total, complete disintegration when he turned her on her stomach and entered her from the back, and when he made her hold his member, now slick, wet and cruel, made her hold it in the palms of her hands, hold it tight, and renew its life. Her teeth chattered from a cold whose ferocity surprised her. But she did not disappear. And when he was through with her, and he rose to rearrange his clothes, she managed to whisper, "I'll tell Lincoln," and he said, "I'll deny it. Who do you think he'll believe? I'm his friend, you're just his woman."

Pearl lay on the sofa after Raj left, paralyzed with fear, too terrified to move, silently watching the darkness filling the rooms. Then around ten o'clock she finally got up. She took a shower and called Macon. But Courtland told her Macon was in Mississippi doing research for her thesis. She did not think to call the police. Who would believe her? And in the days before Lincoln's return she realized she could not tell him. She could not say what Raj had done. Pretense. Make believe. Fabrication. Her personal history was built on triangular towers of deceit. No wonder she'd become an actress. She'd been lying all her life.

LINCOLN RETURNED excited, filled with stories of the balmy West Coast. He told Pearl he had received several offers that he wanted to spend some time considering. She said she was happy for him. She said everything had been fine while he was away, but he was dismayed to find that she had started drinking again in his absence. And he did not know why. She slept fitfully beside him at night, and he found her one morning, huddled on the bathroom floor, shivering, her face streaked with tears. And she was suddenly afraid to be in the apartment alone. Yet when he pressed, asking over and over if there wasn't something she wanted to tell him, she said no, everything was fine.

They didn't have much longer. Lincoln knew that now. When

telling Pearl about his time in L.A., he'd told her about directors, screenwriters he'd met, projects he'd been offered. But he hadn't told her about the hours spent in his hotel room alone, stretched out on his bed, wondering why he should return to her. He went through the meetings and discussions over lunch, dinner, drinks, the whole time, on automatic. Lincoln read the body language and facial expressions of the men he met, for bullshit, deception and promises they most likely could not keep. Sure, he wanted to work on scripts for Hollywood. Why not? But he wasn't going to kiss ass, shuffle or sell the part of his soul New York hadn't devoured yet. And through all the talk, one moment promising, the next inconclusive, he thought about Pearl.

They were locked in a dance that they had both mastered, and which, with the repetition of each step, felt more and more to Lincoln like death. He loved her. And she was killing him. Her silence. Her scars. Her refusal to once and for all let him inside where it was cold and windswept, but where, if she relaxed her vigilance, she need not be alone. Alone, encased in a history that imprisoned her and that she clung to, was who she was the day they met. It was who she remained.

He thought her life on the stage would save her. It merely momentarily obscured the horror of the past. Lying on his hotel bed, night after night, in L.A., Lincoln realized he had to leave the woman he loved if he was going to live. He knew this, feeling it slam into him like a wall. What he didn't know was how he was going to say good-bye.

And now, she could audition, study her lines and get hired for a role, all while she was drunk. Drunk, she now knew, was not always the sloppy, mumbling, awful, falling down out of control syndrome she'd seen in the movies. She could be attentive, articulate, funny, thoughtful, while drunk and most times nobody knew. But Lincoln knew. He could see it in her eyes, in the slight, endless trembling of her hands, in the furtive way she walked around the apartment as though her whole existence was something she wished she could hide in the nearest closet. No, nobody could tell. But him.

She forgot nothing, remembered everything. The remembering, after she was sober, was worse than before. Finally Lincoln confronted her, saying to Pearl one night when she was in the kitchen washing dishes, while he sat at the kitchen table, "I won't stay with a drunk. If you want to destroy yourself, go ahead. Feel free. But you're fucking up my life too, and I won't let you do that."

They were almost like strangers since his return. Standing at the sink, soap bubbles up to her elbows, Pearl heard him confirm what she already knew; he didn't love her. How could he? They hadn't had sex in weeks, because she had been afraid for him to touch her. She found herself barely speaking to him because she didn't know what to say. Lincoln stayed at the theater a lot now, where he had an office. She was once again pounding the streets, looking for work from one end of town to the other, and was often asleep when Lincoln got home.

"I won't have it, Pearl, I just won't have it."

She heard him shouting this, as though the liquor was killing him instead of her, as though *he* were the one who woke trembling and afraid, who went to sleep the same way.

Pearl dried her hands on a towel and sat at the table across from him, seeing judgment and pain in the eyes that, she remembered distinctly, had once long ago, gazed at her with something like love.

"You're betraying everything I thought you were working for," he said evenly, sternly. "Your talent, our future." Listening to him, it struck Pearl as perfect, inevitable, that he would say betray, for she had never trusted him with her heart, or her love.

"Why, Pearl, why?" he finally asked. And she sat before him dumb, mute as a child.

"It helps me forget," she said, after a long while.

"You can't live life as an amnesiac, or is that what you want?" And when she didn't answer, Lincoln told her, "Pearl, I'll give you six months to straighten out your life. Six months and that's it."

Then she found her voice, found it suddenly, totally, fully. "Six months! Six months! To do what? I never promised you I was perfect. I'm not really a character in one of your plays, Lincoln, who you can force to cry, laugh, grow up, walk straight into the ending you choose. I think you've got me confused. Sometimes I'm Jessie Foster, sometimes I'm Pearl Moon, but I'm me. Take your six months and go to hell."

In the aftermath of this fight, Lincoln put it all together. Figured it out, though what he suspected depended much more on feeling, instinct, than fact. He noticed how whenever Raj called, and Pearl answered the phone, she refused to say his name, handing Lincoln the phone as though the receiver was a dead animal. When he talked about the theater, complained about Raj, he could feel Pearl withdraw, pull back something tangible. He invited Raj to the apartment and for the first time ever, he refused to come. And when he asked Pearl to stop by the theater one evening, she told him, "I can't. I just can't ever again."

When all the pieces fell together, like cowrie shells in the sand, he didn't know exactly what to feel, because he was unsure what had really happened. He only knew that if it involved Pearl and Raj, it had been awful.

Since Malika and Fundi had moved out, Raj had begun to hole up in his house, not coming to the theater for days at a time, trying to track down his children, whom he was determined to take from their mothers. The afternoon Lincoln went to see him, he felt ill at ease, on edge, and stood thumbing through a pile of magazines on a table in the hallway, as he asked, feigning a casualness he did not feel, "Did something happen between you and Pearl while I was away?"

"Happen? What do you mean happen?" Raj asked, turning away from Lincoln, entering the living room.

"Like an argument, a disagreement of some kind?"

"Naw, brother, why you ask? She say something?" Raj asked, now settled on the sofa.

"That's just it. Every time I mention your name she gets uptight. And she told me she couldn't come by the theater ever again. Now why would she say that?" Lincoln walked into the living room, still refusing to sit, feeling more in control through the sheer act of remaining on his feet.

"Man, the sister's tripping. You know women. Maybe she *imagined* something. Took me serious when I was joking," Raj laughed huskily, shaking his head in bemused disbelief at the possibility.

"Did you touch her, Raj?"

"Touch her? Touch Pearl?"

"Don't shit me, man, please don't do that," Lincoln said, walking closer to the sofa.

"That's *your* woman."

"Yeah, and I come back from L.A. and she's terrified to be where you are or even to hear your name, and I'm supposed to ignore that? Just tell me what you did. Who said what. What happened?" Lincoln asked reasonably.

"You crazy, man. What are you accusing me of?" Raj sprang from the sofa, belligerence crackling in his voice.

"What're you denying?"

Suddenly, he was pushing Raj, his palms flat, hard against the man's broad chest. And to his surprise, Raj didn't move, just murmured softly, "I don't want to hit you, Lincoln."

"What did you do, Raj? Did you beat her like Malika? Did you touch her?" Lincoln shouted.

"No, man, I didn't, I swear."

Lincoln looked deeply, for the last time, in Raj's eyes. Pearl had tried to warn him long ago, but he had brushed her fears aside. He had chosen to ignore the intuition in Pearl that had sometimes saved them and never let them down. Still, after all that, he had failed her, left her exposed. And so she had said nothing. Denied him even this. Denied what he could see embedded in Raj's eyes. In this moment he hated them both.

Lincoln's fist slammed against Raj's chin, slitting the skin on his knuckles. Raj fell onto the sofa, like a tree plummeting onto a forest floor. He lay rubbing his face, cursing Lincoln, vainly trying to rise. Instinctively, Lincoln cradled his fist in his left hand, looked in amazement at what he had just done and turned and left the house.

But the knowledge merely granted them a reprieve. For the etiquette that bound them required him to say nothing, to nestle against, not challenge Pearl's silence. And for a while things improved. And beneath the canopy of silence which spread over them like a protective sky, there were days even weeks now and then when they recaptured what they sometimes had at the start, but it never lasted. He made two more trips to L.A., for story consultations, he told her, and then in the summer he said he was going out there to spend a few months. He was working on a script he'd been offered, and he needed to be close to the studio. Despite everything, he asked her again to come with him. She responded by saying, "Since you'll just be gone a few months, I'll wait here."

Pearl did indeed wait, although she soon knew she was not really waiting for Lincoln's return. He didn't call this time, but sent her numerous postcards that she didn't answer. Eventually, the postcards became shorter and shorter and then stopped coming at all.

THE CALL CAME at 2 A.M. and Macon let the phone ring. The jagged, nearly psychotic sound of the rings finally slit the seams of her sleep. She was afraid to answer, yet she felt that she must. She lay for some time, hoping that Courtland would awaken and answer it, but when he continued to snore deeply and persistently beside her, Macon reached over him to the bed stand and picked up the receiver. Pearl's voice, wrenching, yet amazingly clear, summoned her from the possibility of sleep or repose for the remainder of the night. Pearl kept saying over and over, "He's not coming back, he's not coming back."

"Who are you talking about, Pearl?" Macon asked.

"Lincoln, he's gone." Her sudden intake of breath sounded like a sob.

"Gone where?"

"Gone for good. I drove him away."

Macon took the phone into the living room and listened to Pearl for the next hour. Her recitation of her fears was morbid, confused, yet in the framework of her life, completely plausible, Macon knew.

"I'm alone and I'm afraid," Pearl said over and over. "I've never been alone like this before. Never."

The careening, off-center sound of Pearl's voice prompted Macon to ask her if she had taken any pills. Pearl said she had not but kept repeating over and over, "I'm alone now, I'm all alone." Macon promised that she would come to New York right away, catch the first plane she could get.

Now she sat heading to New York. She had roused Courtland from sleep at 6 A.M. to tell him what had happened, where she was going. He had mumbled a groggy good-bye. She had asked him to call school and cancel the class she was scheduled to teach. She might have to cancel classes for the rest of the week, depending on what she found in New York.

She was nearing completion on her doctorate and teaching at Simmons College. Two years earlier she had been awarded a Ford Foundation grant to conduct a study of the impact of the civil rights movement on the lives of a group of young girls growing up in three Mississippi towns. The study had required frequent trips to Mississippi but Macon was now in the midst of writing her findings, which would be the basis for her thesis.

On the weekends, twice a month she volunteered to spend twenty-four hours in a battered women's shelter in Cambridge, and had been having long conversations by phone with several women from her movement days who wanted to form a national black feminist organization. It was not lost on her that the dynamism and purpose that characterized her professional and political life were sporadic in her marriage. She had fought so hard for political change that she could not understand why she did not feel the same desire to fight for her marriage.

When he finished Harvard Law, Courtland took a job with Legal Aid, turning down the lucrative offers from law firms looking for overqualified token blacks. But he felt defeated by the hopelessness of his clients and the bureaucracy he had to deal with to get them help. So Courtland became increasingly involved with a group of black Boston politicians and community activists who were concerned with issues of police brutality and low income housing for the poor. He journeyed to the south several times a year, to visit his mother and to gauge the political situation in the new south, the south that had produced a liberal Georgia peanut farmer who looked like he had a good chance of becoming president.

It was hard for Macon to say when she had first felt them losing it, losing what had kept them together. She was terrified of the idea that perhaps, in the end, it was the movement that had kept them together, that without that they had nothing. She could not remember the last time they had gone to a movie or out to dinner or talked about something that was totally inconsequential. They had spent their married life fighting various political battles and had lost the marriage in the process, it seemed.

She had no idea what Courtland's favorite color was, or his favorite meal. They were so busy studying or organizing that they ate Chinese takeout, or microwaved something out of the freezer most nights. Courtland often left his offices at Legal Aid and went straight to a community meeting that might not end until eleven or twelve. The marriage had been a studied, consistent movement toward progress and freedom. But for whom? More and more Macon found herself just wanting to lie on a beach somewhere beside her husband, yet she was afraid to because she had no idea what she would or could say to him in a setting like that. The women at the shelters came in bruised, beaten, battered. They were beaten because they didn't prepare a meal fast enough, or because they had not been obedient enough, or because their husbands had seen the seeds of betrayal in a friendly smile given to a stranger. These women had been battered because their existence, their femaleness, set husbands, boyfriends, on edge, inflamed them with doubt about who they were.

Leaving the shelter exhausted, drained by her shift, Macon drove home remembering that she and Courtland had not argued in months, or was it years? They had no time for the accumulation of discontents, the small brushfires of anger, to spread and consume them. She wanted to raise her voice sometimes in passionate release of some emotion held dear, to argue and then make up by making love, hating and loving all at once, all jumbled together in a solid, terrible mass that was sometimes love too.

Maybe it had started to fall apart when they found out, as she had long suspected, that she could not conceive. Courtland had started talking about children last year. Since Macon would be finished with her doctorate soon and Courtland had plans to set up his own practice, they agreed that now was the time to start a family. When they found out about her problem, she suggested adoption. But he did not want to adopt. He had looked at Macon and said, "I want my own child, not somebody else's." Macon took the words as a kind of declaration of war, for they now knew that he could not have *his own* child with her.

It had all come to a head during the drive home from the doctor's office. Courtland was staring straight ahead, as though afraid even to look at her. The silence between them was the worst she had ever known. Earlier, as she walked beside him on the way to the car, Macon had already shifted to a solution to the problem, refusing to let the situation imprison or derail her. Fifteen minutes into the ride home, she suggested that they consider adoption. That's when Courtland had looked at her then as they sat stopped before a red light, and said, "I want my own child not somebody else's." She sat biting her lip to keep the tears from falling. She would not let him see her cry, could not, no matter what. For years they had had long talks with their friends about how important it was to adopt the black children warehoused in foster care. They had talked about the need for the black community to take care of its own.

During the time they had tried to have a child, and approached lovemaking as an act of faith and renewal, Macon had often wondered what their child would look like, what kind of mother she would be. She joked with Courtland, as they lay in each other's arms, about reading the Fourteenth and Fif-

teenth Amendments to the Constitution to their child at bed-
time. He had laughed at the stunning perfection of that idea.
Macon was sure they were happy.

And then, when it wasn't to be, she was utterly surprised at
how much it had mattered to her to be a mother. While Courtland felt he could only be a father to his specific seed, Macon
was eager to love any motherless child. Her husband had left
her with no way out, no way to win.

BY THE TIME the plane arrived in New York, Macon was
plagued by a distress that congealed in her stomach and
pounded in her head. How would she comfort Pearl? What
would she say?

She found Pearl drained but coherent and she told Macon
everything, about Raj and the break with Lincoln. Macon sat
on Pearl's bed amid the rumpled sheets, the close, humid air of
the room pressing around her, and stifled a sob as she listened
to Pearl's story. The rape horrified her, and she was not surprised when her efforts to convince Pearl to press charges, even
now, months after the fact, failed.

"I'm terrified, Macon. I've never been on my own before, not
since Lincoln and I met. I've never been on my own at all."

"It's easier then you think, being on your own," Macon said
bitterly, flash-forwarding to visions of herself alone. Lately, she
had been haunted by her own fear of the future. "Lincoln
wasn't your Svengali, Pearl, he was your lover. You can go on
and you will. Everything he taught you, everything you
learned, you'll use it now, because you have to."

"But, Macon, I'm not sure I want to go on. With any of it. The acting, living, feeling. I live only when I'm onstage, Macon. It's the only life I have."

"It's the only life you want, Pearl, and it wasn't enough for Lincoln. There wasn't enough room for him on that stage you've erected in your head."

"Why should I go on, Macon, why?"

"You'll go on, Pearl, with all of it. Because you're just like me. No matter how much I think I want to die, sometimes, it's moments like this that convince me the only thing I can do is live.

THEY MADE A list of all the people Pearl knew in the city and Pearl was amazed at the number of her contacts, in her work, people she could go to for money, for advice, for a job to tide her over.

That evening Macon took a bubble bath while Pearl sat on the toilet plaiting her hair. Slowly, Macon began to tell her about her inability to conceive, and about Courtland's reaction.

"And, Pearl, you know, it hurts, it hurts so bad." Her face was haggard, bewildered. She reached for the glass of white wine on the floor beside the tub.

"Because of Courtland?"

"No, because of me. Why was I working all this time to make the world a better place, if it wasn't to make it safe for a child?"

"But, Macon, the world isn't safe," Pearl said emphatically.

"I know, it never will be, but hell, I've done my part. I've cleared a patch of ground where my child could stand in pride and dignity. I earned that for it."

"Are you saying you feel incomplete?" Pearl asked.

"Don't try that game on me," Macon said angrily, draining the glass of wine and handing it to Pearl.

"I wanted a child," she said defiantly, sinking lower in the tub, a wave of bubbles rising to her ears. "I wanted to teach, to write, to love my husband, save the world, be your friend and somebody's mama too. Hell, Pearl, I don't feel incomplete, but I do feel cheated."

Macon raised her leg and watched the water, soap and bubbles, glistening and fresh, slide slowly down her leg. "I had more love in my heart, Pearl, than I knew," she said, easing her leg back into the water. "And I feel it inside me now about to burst. My husband doesn't want it. What'll I do?"

"What'll happen when you go back?" Pearl asked. "To you and Courtland?"

"I don't know, Pearl. I only know I can't continue to live stalemated, with my dreams on hold."

Macon stayed five days and during that time, she took Pearl down to Macy's and they bought new curtains, new sheets and pillows and new pictures for the walls. The night before her departure, Macon told Pearl, "Only one person lives here now and that person is you. But just because there's only you here, doesn't mean you're alone. You're only alone if you want to be. Will you remember that?"

"I will," Pearl promised. "Macon, I will."

PEARL SAT staring at her face under the unforgiving glare of the harsh fluorescent bulbs rimming the dressing table mirror. Skillfully, meticulously, she applied makeup, as though headed for the stage, rather than a dinner with Lincoln Sturgis.

Only in the last year had she been able to look at herself in the mirror without flinching. Her thick, willful dreadlocks, tied back from her face by a green and gold swath of cloth, were home to gleaming, slender threads of gray that had arrived presumptuously, prematurely, when she stopped drinking. At first, she had tried pulling the gray hairs out, then she tried dying her hair, but in both cases, the gray grew back triumphant, sturdier than before. So Pearl had called a truce and found a kind of poetry in the combination of her gray hair and the still staunch youthfulness of her face.

It was an odd face, a face that would always tell on her. Tiny crow's-feet pinched the skin around her eyes, whispering to anyone who looked closely, "I used to be a drunk." At some point, the makeup had to come off, the sun had to come up, the lights had to be turned on; then you got stared at straight on, with no possibility of retreat. Yet her face still contained—no matter how fleetingly, the questing, startling innocence that nothing had been able to destroy.

Time had passed as though it were capital squandered in an overnight binge of gambling. The future arrived and became the past, Pearl now knew, whether you were ready for it or not. She looked at the array of eye shadows lined up before her in the makeup case and chose the color that matched the green and gold dress she was wearing. When Lincoln had called and told her he was coming to town on business and wanted to take her out to dinner, she had spent three days searching in her favorite boutiques for this dress.

Tonight she would be beautiful. She would hide every trace of anything ugly, terrible, all the things she convinced herself she couldn't remember, in order to survive.

The rape had congealed, hard and unmovable in her memory. There were times when it festered, aching and sore, throwing a curtain between her and the rest of the world. Other times, most times, it lay ticking, synchronized and lethal, its poisonous qualities camouflaged by an inert exterior. She had done well in the years since the break with Lincoln, the horror with Raj, that's what she told herself. There had been numerous national and local TV commercials. She had performed each summer for the past three years in Joseph Papp's Shakespeare in the Park productions. And she had acted steadily on the stage in New York and on tour around the country. A one-woman show on the life of Ida B. Wells, which she had put together with Macon's help and that of a writer she met through Simone, had taken Pearl to college campuses across the country during Black History Month. But best of all, she was beginning her second year as a defense attorney on a highly acclaimed TV courtroom drama.

Pearl played Jasmine Holloway, a dreadlock-wearing (because she had insisted on keeping hers and the director wanted her for the part badly enough to say yes), politically savvy lawyer. Pearl had fought with the scriptwriter all the first season for a lover for Jasmine. When shooting started next week, Jasmine Holloway would be the only black woman on prime-time TV who would have an almost nude sex scene with her lover. And if Pearl had anything to do with it, she would try to get more than one scene like that written into the script this year. There had been a time when she could hardly bear to go to the movies or watch television. The roles for black women had hardened into stock roles of prostitute, caretaker or confidante to a major white character. Pearl looked back over her career and could not remember once having played a love interest.

She had done well. The need to defy her designation as damaged goods had propelled Pearl to work with furious determination. Several years ago she had decided that if there was a role to be had she would get it. When there was no work, she would make some. She cultivated directors, casting agents, made peace with former enemies, prayed, whatever was required.

Her most transcendent, fulfilling moments still occurred on stage. She had to work if she was to do more than just survive. Macon had told her that it wasn't as hard as it seemed to be alone. But it was. She continued to choose men, when she allowed them in her life, who would dominate or direct her. Her relationships were most often short, intense, unsatisfying affairs, ending in recriminations, fraught with scenes as full blown and traumatic as anything she played on the stage. She had become a master at approaching her life as a script she had been handed that still needed work. When emotions got messy, or out of control, there was either an intermission or a denouement. Soon the scene ended, the run was over.

All this was convenient, efficient, and left Pearl's soul as thirsty and parched as a stretch of desert sand. There had been two abortions. And several months ago she had had her tubes tied. While Macon had tried to make the world safe for a child, Pearl knew the world never would be. Never. All she had to do was look at her own life to see that.

Yes, that color would do. It would do fine, she thought, as she applied the eye liner and then the lash builder. She was starring in a play when she fell off the edge, a drama in which she was a murder victim. She died six nights a week. That's how she thought of the role. Slowly, she had been requiring more and more alcohol to sustain the numbness she needed to get through each day and to separate herself emotionally from the character she played.

Each night, she had to give raging, potent life to a young woman who became the victim of a gang assault. The play hit so close to home that there were days when Pearl felt she could not go on stage. Still she dredged up the backlog of her own pain to give one of her most powerful performances. In the third week of the run, with the house packed every night, she suddenly could not go on stage. She had been drinking heavily all day, feeling morose and brooding over the ways in which her character had begun to infest her own thoughts, echoing an end for herself that had haunted her imagination for as long as she could remember. At the very moment that she was to walk onto the stage, she could not move. She stood paralyzed, voices reigning in her head that told her if she stepped on the stage, she would die, this time for real. Her understudy went on and she resigned from the production and checked into Bellevue, showing signs of exhaustion. That's when her doctor told her she had to stop drinking. Stop drinking or die, he'd said, as though the latter prospect was supposed to frighten her. He didn't know how close she had come to choosing it.

She told no one, not Macon, not Mae Ann, that she was in Bellevue. She lay in the narrow bed, terrified, some days hoping she would never have to move again; other days, suicidal at the thought that she might not ever act again. During her hospitalization, her brother Junior was killed, shot in an alley in Jackson, Mississippi, in a fight over one hundred and fifty dollars' worth of heroin. When she left Bellevue and returned home, the telegram informing her of his death was the first thing she saw when she entered the foyer. It had been shoved under her door more than two weeks before.

For a year Pearl attended Alcoholics Anonymous, listening to the stories of the people in the meetings, their tales of defeat and humiliation, sure that she was different, convinced that they were stupid or just plain unlucky. When she did stop drinking, she stopped not so much because she wanted to live, but because she wanted to continue to act. She auditioned for a role in a new play by a veteran, award-winning playwright.

The play was to be the major drama of the fall theater season and was to be nontraditionally cast, fully integrated. But after her audition the director pulled her aside and told her that he had heard about her drinking, her hospitalization. She was the one he wanted to hire, but he just couldn't take a chance on her. That's when she stopped. She hadn't had a drink since.

FINALLY SATISFIED with what she saw in the mirror, Pearl stood and reached for the new dress. As she examined her figure, Pearl smoothed the dress around her hips and stomach. She was weak with anticipation and excitement. In the years since their breakup she and Lincoln had talked often, but she had always managed to be out of town or unavailable when he came to New York. Taking one last look in the mirror, Pearl smiled with genuine delight, certain that before the night was over she would be in Lincoln's arms once again. If asked, she could not have said, however, what she expected to find there.

WORDS HARDLY mattered anymore. Once he had used language as exorcism and explanation. He had thought words were incorruptible, sacred. But that was before Hollywood taught him how cheap, and even sinister, language could be. He was a script doctor now, overhauling the unworkable, the unredeemable, pulling it all together, pumping the requisite humor, drama, violence, into stories too expensive to write off.

Lincoln didn't know whether he was a hired gun or a hired hand. He had reached the mid-six figures and he still felt each paycheck was an act of theft. The endless story conferences, the team editing, the intrusion of brand-name actors and brand-name directors into the process, threatened every time to defeat him. Six figures for what? After the bastardization of his dialogue, the cannibalization of his ideas, what was left? Six figures for fourteen lines? He had written a script on the life of Paul Robeson that was locked in the safe deposit box in his bank in L.A. He hadn't shown it to anybody. He didn't know if he ever would.

He kept waiting, finally, to be happy. He was holding his breath, waiting to exhale and breathe in contentment. He had married and would soon be a father but he felt more trepidation than joy. He had spent years trying to get over Pearl; to conquer the feeling that it had all been a waste, she a hopeless case, he a fool.

He had waited all that time, all those years, for her to love him. When he finally left, he tried so hard to forget her. But he could not. Something of her echoed in the manner of all the women after her. He called her every few months, afraid that without him she'd crumble, some part of him hoping that was true. Clutching the phone during those calls, he waited to hear her say she needed him, to come back. He waited, viciously, angrily sometimes, to hear her say nothing had been right since he left. Oddly enough, he never expected to hear her say she loved him; that was too much to ask. But she hadn't crumbled. Her talent hadn't disintegrated, rather it had spiraled into a thunderous shout that drowned out whatever personal demons had tried to bring her down. He sometimes wondered painfully, what would have happened to them if he had stayed? Where would they be, if she could have loved him?

"You look great!" Lincoln said, as Pearl settled in the booth where he sat waiting for her. He leaned over the table and kissed her gently on the cheek, his eyes gazing with approval on what he saw.

"And you, you look . . ."

"Older," Lincoln finished for her, laughing broadly.

"Older, but great," she told him. Pearl knew she was blushing but she didn't care. Being face to face with Lincoln again made her feel wonderful and she wanted never to stop smiling. His face was heavier. Pearl had seen evidence of a paunch when she sat down. He had shaved his beard and heavy bags were lodged beneath his eyes, but he looked healthy and prosperous.

Lincoln reached for Pearl's hands and caressed her fingers. Each time he tried to speak, he found himself unable to find the words. Finally he said simply, "Pearl, it's been too long. Way too long."

"I know." And she meant it.

"There were times when I felt like you were hiding from me. You were always conveniently out of town or indisposed when I came back. You weren't hiding, were you? Not from me?"

"Would you forgive me if I was?"

"I'd forgive you if you'd help me to understand why you avoided me."

Pearl eased her fingers from Lincoln's hold and said, "I just wanted our reunion to come at the right time, the right time for both of us."

This admission saddened Lincoln, Pearl could tell. He shifted in his seat, moved his gaze from her face to his glass of bourbon.

"It was never about that with us, not then, not now," he said quietly.

The waiter came and asked Pearl what she would like to drink.

"Soda water is fine," she said. When the waiter departed, she told Lincoln, "I haven't had a drink in five years."

"Was it hard to stop?" he asked.

"Everything was at stake, Lincoln, I had no choice," Pearl said.

"I wish you could have stopped when we were still together. Who knows what might have happened?" Lincoln said. There was an awkward, though not uncomfortable pause before he said, raising his glass, "Congratulations on your sobriety and on the show. I'm one of your biggest fans."

"We just got renewed for next year."

"I've been hearing wonderful things about you."

"Every time I pick up *Jet* I see you," she joked. "But tell me, how is it out there? I know you've been doing scripts and I saw the two films you directed."

"You want to know what it's like?" Lincoln asked, taking a swig of his bourbon. "I got out of Mississippi and the movement without a scratch. I managed to remain nonviolent in the face of ignorant, red-necked sheriffs, but last week I got into a fight with a man who sits behind a desk as big as this room just because his uncle owns the studio. That's how it is."

"But what about the scripts?"

"I've written a dozen, but only two have been made into films. It's frustrating. The films I directed didn't do well—the reviews didn't translate into box office—and, Pearl, they never forgive or forget lost profit out there, *never*."

"I heard you'd directed some TV."

"Now and then. Here and there," he shrugged.

"So, will you be directing the play? How'd the meetings go today?"

"You know, it's like negotiating the Paris Peace talks. Today

145

it looks possible, tomorrow, who knows. . . . Did you hear about Raj's death?" he asked.

"Yes."

"I read about it in the *Herald-Tribune* in Heathrow Airport," he told her, wondering how she felt talking about Raj, thinking about him, feeling his own pulse quicken, his own skin grow warm at the memory of Raj's face when he hit him, the bruised, battered feeling that had invaded his fist. He had changed and saved nothing that day.

"I know something happened between you two, Pearl," he began, unable to look at her as he said this. "I've always known. I never knew exactly what happened. I only knew it was terrible for you."

"Lincoln, please let's talk about something else. Anything else." Pearl nervously looked at the other tables, wondering if the other patrons could hear what they were saying, if they could see the shame that had branded her instantly, the moment Lincoln said his name. If she could have disappeared without moving, run, without leaving her seat, she would have been gone. This wasn't the script she had rehearsed, imagined, conjured in her head the past week. These weren't the words she had daydreamed they would exchange. She could still hear Lincoln, going on, despite her plea for him to stop.

"And I never told you, but I should have, how sorry I am for letting you down. I feel responsible in some way. I didn't listen to you. And I should have. But it hurt me so much, when you didn't tell me. After that, Pearl, I felt like there was nothing for me to do but leave."

"I couldn't tell you then, Lincoln, and I can't tell you now. Anyway, that's the past, it's over," she said, her voice rising, arching, straining for a confidence she would have to marshal to carry her through the rest of the evening. Taking a deep breath, she said, "I read about your marriage. Congratulations. Are you happy?

"I am," he lied. "Are you?"

"Yes," she lied, too.

THEY GOSSIPED about actors and directors they knew. Lincoln told her anecdotes about the Hollywood stars he had met and worked with. They reminisced. In the end, it was this trivial, nonthreatening talk about others that salvaged the evening. When they finished dessert Pearl told Lincoln, "I've come up in the world, I want you to see my new place."

"Sure, where is it?"

"West End Avenue."

"That's a long way from Harlem, baby," Lincoln grinned.

"Not so far," she said, returning his smile.

Pearl now lived in a modern twenty-story apartment building. On the way up to the fifteenth floor, she and Lincoln stood in a corner of the elevator with their arms wrapped around each other. In her apartment, Lincoln admired the sleek modern furniture, the framed prints on the wall and the huge art books on the coffee table. An hour later, they had finished cups of coffee and lay in each other's arms on the sofa, when Pearl suddenly remembered, "And I've got this great view, I want you to see it."

But before she could move from the sofa, he pulled her back toward him, saying, "You're the only view I want to see tonight."

It was as though they had just kissed yesterday. "I never forgot you. I never did," Lincoln said. "Do you know how many times I wanted to come back, to start all over again?" He was unbuttoning the back of her dress and Pearl was helping him out of his jacket. "But I was afraid you'd tell me to go away. You were always pushing me away, Pearl. But in my whole life, I've never found anyone like you." Pearl reached across to turn off the lamp. In the dark, Lincoln pushed down her pantyhose and opened her bra, burying his face in her soft breasts. As she threw his shirt across the room and reached down to expertly remove his underpants, she said, "I'm sorry, Lincoln, I'm just so sorry."

They took one another on the carpeted floor in the living room and against the wall beside the startling view that she had wanted him to see. They slept and then found themselves in Pearl's bed where she recited passages from the plays Lincoln had written for her. Lincoln promised that when he next got the chance to direct he would insist that she be cast in a lead role. They made love and promises into the morning, and woke next to each other as unsure of their relationship as they had been when the previous evening started. Lincoln slipped out of bed and took refuge in the bathroom where he showered and dressed. He opened the bathroom door to find Pearl propped up against the pillows staring straight at him. Lincoln stood in the bathroom door and saw Jessie Foster's eyes and Pearl Moon's trembling, expectant smile. She had survived. Without him. Lincoln sat on the edge of the bed beside Pearl. He held her in his arms. When he started to speak, she placed her fingers on his lips. "Let's just improvise from now on," she said. "There aren't any more roles to play."

Lincoln kissed her and said, "I've got to go."

PASSAGES

WHEN MACON ENTERED the Black Student Union's tiny office, she was too startled to move. She stood reading the word Nigger over and over, its red spray-painted letters, furious and immense, leaping out at her from every wall. She felt sick. But before sickness could overwhelm her, anger staked its claim. Books whose spines had been broken, whose pages had been torn out, lay in a messy pile beside an overturned desk. The posters of Frederick Douglass, Malcolm X and Sojourner Truth lay shredded at her feet, knife cuts scarring each dark face. In the hall behind her, Macon's students stirred, moved once again by the sight of what they had discovered earlier in the day. Finally she walked across the littered floor, retrieving a book from the pile as she sank slowly into a swivel chair.

Stunned, the students huddled outside the entrance to the office, or stood inside the room a few feet away from the walls where the epithet was scrawled. Fisk Randolph, a junior, righted the desk and perched on a corner, nervously kicking his leg. These students, Macon knew, had probably never witnessed anything as heartbreaking as this. Standing before her were the fresh-faced children of the black middle class. Many of them had attended elementary and high school with whites, had dated white girls or boys. When they took her class on the history of the civil rights movement they told Macon that no one had told them the things they were learning. They had been prepared for everything they were meant to encounter in life but this.

"You aren't going to let them get away with this, are you?" Macon asked, scanning the group before her.

"Hell, no," Fisk said eagerly, kicking the edge of the desk. "Ever since I came in this morning and found this, I've been trying to map out a strategic response." Fisk was an honor roll student, majoring in political science, and a star on the basketball team. "I called the student paper, and the president's office."

"I'll call the *Washington Post*," Macon said. "I've got friends there who might be able to cover this. And I'll arrange a meeting with the president."

"I think we need to have a rally," Fisk said, now clearly enthused about the possibilities the incident suggested.

"That's a good idea," Macon said. "It's very important that you go on the offensive, fight back."

"Will you speak at the rally?" Fisk asked.

"Of course. And I'll work on a statement that the rest of the black faculty and staff can sign."

"How will we get this off the walls?" Fisk asked, looking around the room, despair momentarily shadowing his resolve.

"That's the problem of Buildings and Grounds. For right now the Black Student Union needs a new office. And you need one immediately. Tell the president that."

Macon sat with the students for nearly an hour and discussed the strategy for the protest and then one by one they drifted out. The last student to leave was Marva Dunbar, a freshman. While the others were talking, she had busied herself with retrieving the books and papers from the floor, trying to make order out of the chaos of the office. When she and Macon were finally alone she asked, "Why, Professor Fields, why?" She stood before Macon, vainly trying to repair a hardback edition of Frederick Douglass's autobiography that had been torn in half. The young girl's hands simply would not give up as they pieced and gathered the pages into the broken binding. "I have a white roommate, what do I say to her after this?"

"I don't know why, Marva," Macon confessed. "Marva, I really don't. All the books I've read, the books I've written, the political work I've done, and I still don't know why. But I can tell you this; you say what you feel to your roommate, let her know that what happened in this room hurts you and that it should hurt her too."

The girl smiled weakly at these words, which had satisfied Macon even less than they had assured Marva.

"Thanks, Professor," she said, "I'll do that." She picked up her knapsack, slung it over her shoulder and left, still holding the damaged book.

Macon had planned to stay in the office a while longer, to simply sit at the desk, as an act of defiance. But when Marva left the room she stood and gathered her briefcase and books, so chilled was she by the atmosphere in the room. Then her eyes moved to the room's only window. It was cloudy and overcast outside, the weather as brooding and intemperate as she now felt. A vigorous gust of wind swirled the piles of late November leaves in the main yard of the campus.

Incidents like this had occurred at campuses all over the country, at isolated obscure schools and at institutions as prestigious as Amherst and Brown. In response administrators held conferences, conducted surveys and studies, but still nobody could answer satisfactorily the question Marva had asked.

It had been a rough semester. One of Macon's students, a senior, had been killed in the parking lot of a local nightclub, another had attempted suicide. Macon's hand moved instinctively, as it now sometimes did, to the place where her left breast used to be and gently rubbed the spongelike prosthesis beneath her sweater. This reflexive, unconscious action, she had concluded, was the sign of her grieving. Her hand comforted and still wondered why.

MACON TAUGHT sociology at Jefferson College in Fairfax, Virginia, where her students were mostly young and white, produced by worlds so economically and racially homogeneous that, for some, she bordered on the exotic. In each class she required an autobiographical essay and in these papers she found evidence of the tensions riveting these students' worlds.

In her course the Sociology of the Afro-American, the brutal yet unsuspected prejudice, learned at home, mastered at the dinner table, found expression. Her students often incorporated the dangerous, muddled clichés of political candidates into their essays on current events. In the women's sociology course, Macon received accounts of casual, accepted physical and psychological abuse of mothers and daughters; the burdensome, required search for beauty; the still strong hold of romantic love as a censor of impulses that might separate women from their traditional legacy.

Yet each semester there were a handful of students whose intelligence was wedded to a sparkling diligence, whose questions turned Macon's notions and theories inside out, students who turned her, in the face of their questions, into a student.

The few blacks in her classes huddled together like refugees;

a solid united front gathering confidence from one another. They were unknown quantities to their white peers, unexamined and unimagined. In the face of this startling yet mundane indifference they sought solace from each other. They attended a school that had special scholarships for nonwhite students, and various academic support systems in place to ensure their success, yet, it was also a school that, in the last year, had become home to a student white supremacist organization that Macon was certain had ransacked the BSU office.

Macon had found no cloistered, ivory towers at any of the schools where she had taught. Reality was what stared back at her from the eyes of her students, what she found in the politics of various departments.

Despite this, she taught for the same reason she had worked in the movement—to influence the shaping of the world, to thrust her vision and commentary into its flow. Friends had died in the movement, and she taught to honor them.

Macon was a tenured, senior faculty member, the author of 'two respected books, yet, as she left the BSU office and walked across the campus, she felt vulnerable and unsure. Her presence, legitimacy and place in the academy seemed to be always open to question. She felt she had to earn the respect of her colleagues over and over every year. Raising her collar against a sudden brisk wind, Macon realized that she knew the answer to Marva's question, but she had simply lacked the courage to reveal it.

As she neared her car in the parking lot, Macon bumped into Hilton Butler, the energetic head of the Sociology Department.

"Macon, how are you?" he asked.

"Fine, fine," she said, trying to disguise the way she really felt.

"How are you really?" he asked, placing a large hand on her shoulder. "I've heard more convincing lies from my six-year-old."

Tall, bearded, with wavy, wiry blond hair, Hilton possessed the robustness and spirit of a mountain man. Macon had told Hilton about the cancer when she discovered it, swearing him to secrecy, fearing the pity of her colleagues as much as the disease. As far as she knew, he had not violated her confidence.

Macon told Hilton about the ransacking of the BSU office and he asked if there was anything he could do. She suggested a faculty meeting to discuss the incident and to plan ways to discuss it in classes. Hilton agreed.

"I haven't seen you in a while," he complained.

"I've been around, but my classes have been at the same time as faculty meetings."

"Are you still in remission," he asked gently.

"Still."

"Good, I'm rooting for you. . . . Did you get the memo about the dinner at Cassie's house for the candidate from Penn State?"

"I got it."

"Will you be there?"

"Honestly, Hilton, I'll try."

"You can't do more than that. Go home and get some rest."

THE DRIVE FROM Fairfax to Washington where she lived was about forty-five minutes and driving along Route 495 Macon thought of the changes that had occurred in the state of Virginia. She had grown up in Richmond, once the capital of the Confederacy, a city steeped in a stubborn nostalgia for the antebellum world, and crowded with statues and monuments to fallen rebel commanders. Listening to a John Coltrane tape on her car stereo, Macon wondered how well Jefferson Davis and James Madison slept in their graves now that a black man called the governor's mansion home.

THE HOUSE LOOMED around her, reeking of loneliness and neglect. Entering the foyer, Macon set her briefcase and several envelopes from her mailbox on a table in the hallway. Shadows from the sudden arrival of evening filtered in through the sheer curtains at the front door window and intensified the momentary hesitance that frequently gripped her when she entered her house. At times like these, she had an eerie, fleeting desire to go no further. This was the house where she had fought the possibility of death. This was where she had begun to heal, only to find the process more daunting than she had ever imagined. In the living room Macon turned on the light and gazed at the newspapers strewn on the floor beside the sofa, the stacks of videos atop the television set, the yellow legal pads, the books on the coffee table and the coffee mugs on the side tables, as though assessing the handiwork of a stranger.

Once she had been almost fanatically neat. Now she had grown used to the disheveled atmosphere that prevailed in nearly every room of the house. The disorder that once could threaten a headache, now soothed her, took on a presence of its own that she respected. It was merely an extension of her life.

Sitting on the sofa, Macon reached for the remote control and turned on the television, which she kept on now virtually all the time. The face of one of the city's most popular black anchormen sprang into view. Gazing at the screen with the sound off, Macon realized that she was hungry, but the thought of trying to decide what to eat sent waves of fatigue through her. Instead she removed her jacket, tossing it into a nearby chair, and stretched out on the sofa. She would rest a few minutes, she told herself, instantly falling asleep.

Three months after her forty-fourth birthday, Macon discovered the cancer while examining herself after a shower. The hard tiny lump felt like a bullet lodged beneath her skin. A biopsy of the lump revealed that the cancer had spread so rapidly that a modified radical mastectomy was immediately performed followed by chemotherapy. Within a month of discovering the lump, she had only one remaining breast. How, she often wondered, could her body have been plotting to kill her without her knowledge. Except for the tiny lump, she had no other signs of the illness.

Two weeks after the surgery, Macon attended an American Cancer Society seminar on breast prostheses. Entering the room, she saw five tables lined with thirty different types of prostheses on display. There were breasts made of silicone gel, cloth and plastic. There were breasts the color of deep chocolate, breasts with brand names like Bosom Buddy and Nearly Me. How suitable, Macon thought, when she picked up several prostheses shaped like teardrops. The hour spent looking at these prostheses had depressed her so much that she had considered not wearing one at all. Her doctor had not been able to give her a medical argument for its necessity.

She had challenged the conventional wisdom in the classroom and in her life, but, even after a long talk with a friend who had chosen not to wear a prosthesis, Macon had decided to wear one. It changed nothing. She remained a one-breasted woman living with cancer. Yet how important it had become to fool the world, if not herself. Her hair had begun to grow back and she had symbolically burned the wig she'd had to wear during the chemotherapy treatments. She was determined not to have to wear one again.

Pearl stayed with her for a time during the worst of the ordeal, which Macon now recalled as the entire time. Macon, so independent, so self-sufficient, had subtly tried to resist Pearl's competent, nurturing hand. But after a while, her protests that she was fine had exhausted her. During the chemotherapy treatments after the operation, she was home for three months.

While watching a movie on TV one night, Pearl turned to look at Macon during a commercial and said, "It's only a tittie. That's all they took. A tittie."

"But it was *my* tittie, mine," Macon said, feeling the inevitable, hot tears well quickly in her eyes. Pearl hugged her gently and Macon thought, It wouldn't be just a tittie to you.

As an actress Pearl valued her body, her looks; she cherished her physique, her attractive face. How she depended on it, even as she had sought to destroy it over the years with alcohol and men.

"I wasn't making light of what's happened," Pearl apologized, turning off the television and huddling at the foot of Macon's bed. "I was just trying to put it in perspective."

"I know, I know," Macon said.

"At AA," Pearl began carefully, "they told me I'd have to learn to love what I'd been through—waking up with a head the size of this room, the crow's-feet around my eyes from the alcohol fucking with my veins—I'd have to learn to look back on all that as just *stuff* that had my name on it, that belonged to me and my past but that couldn't claim me now. You'll have to learn to love that empty spot on your chest. Besides, you've been more scared than you are now, I

159

know. Tell me something that scared you as much as what you're facing now."

"It's not just having one breast, it's the cancer, it could come back."

"Tell me," Pearl insisted. Macon stared at the walls, her lips pursed tight, as though reigning in a potential explosion, and refused to speak.

Pearl said, "When I had my second abortion a couple of years ago, I thought if I have to go through this again I will die. The anesthesia always took me out. I felt like I was having DT's. And with this last abortion, it took me a long time to come out from under the drugs. I felt like I was stuck inside this dark horrible tunnel."

"When that dog bit me outside the courthouse in Greenwood," Macon said slowly. She coughed and wiped her eyes with a tissue. Sinking back against the pillows, she said, "Believe me, girl, I was scared. That business about your life passing before your eyes is true. I was only what, twenty? There wasn't much life to recall but it zipped by when that dog's teeth sank into my right arm. I'd never felt such terror."

"Terror, my dear," Pearl pronounced solemnly, "is also the first day of sobriety, the longest most gruesome day of your life."

THEY SAT UP the remainder of that night, trading horror stories, sharing near misses. The retelling of stories they both already knew—old miseries, old defeats, redefined that which made them friends.

Pearl had helped Macon pick out a wig when her hair began to fall out because of the chemo, turning the wig-hunting expedition into a farce, prancing around the shop in a suburban mall, assuming a different identity to match each wig. It was Pearl who was there when Macon was sick to her stomach from the chemo, holding her head while she wretched in the bathroom and it was Pearl who cleaned up after her as if she were a baby.

MACON WOKE UP still tired, still hungry. When she turned on her answering machine, there was a message from Courtland. He was coming to Washington next week, and wanted to drop by to see her, he said. She had finally reached a point where she could be in the same room with Courtland and not feel herself drenched in regret. It had taken a long time but she liked to think they'd backtracked to the beginning and were friends as at the start. The last year of their marriage had been a protracted stalemate that neither possessed the courage or good will to break. Macon had wanted to adopt a child and shape a marriage that included greater intimacy, the possibility for surprise. Courtland insisted that he could only father his own child and that his political work was still paramount. The divorce was the only thing they were able to agree on in the end. After it was over, Courtland returned to Mississippi where he had been marshaling support for a run for Congress.

For several years after the divorce she had thought about adopting a child. She had gone so far as to make inquiries with public and private agencies. But the depth, the weight of the need of the children she saw overwhelmed her. They had been battered, beaten, born to drug-addicted mothers, shunted from one often abusive foster home to another. Their need for love and stability struck Macon as bottomless. She gave nearly a dozen lectures during the school year at colleges around the country. Her research required frequent travel, sometimes abroad. The world had become her village. What would she alone, with no partner to lean on for help, be able to give to a child who needed someone who could always be there? If she were married, if her life were more predictable, if she could afford and live with the decision to hire live-in help—the ifs piled up around her desire to adopt and soon left it quietly buried under a blanket of doubt.

There was also a message on her machine from Noble Carson. He was at a meeting he said but wanted to stop by to see her that evening. He would call back later to see if she was in.

THEY HAD GONE out for dinner twice in the last month. The sound of Noble's voice on the machine filled Macon with a familiar mixture of fear and desire. It had been a long time since she was involved with a man.

Around the time she discovered the lump, there had been the beginnings of an affair with a black dean at Jefferson College. When she found out about the cancer she simply told him that everything had changed; she could no longer see him. She had not even given him a decent explanation; she had felt that her disease allowed her to be thoughtless and rude. She did not care about his feelings or his sincere hurt when she hung up abruptly during a call to see how she was.

During the actual battle against cancer, her body had been poked and probed so much that the thought of a man's touch had totally dismayed her. But since the doctor had confirmed that she was in remission, she had continued to live a life of celibacy. First, she had not wanted to be touched, then when

Macon realized she was out of harm's way, she wanted to avoid the emotional disarray and confusion that love always seemed to bring. But in the wake of Noble's promise to call her tonight, she felt desire stir in the pit of her groin, unmistakable and full-fledged.

NOBLE CARSON was one of the first people Macon met when she moved to Washington. She knew him before his divorce, before his fall from grace, before his time in prison. An aide to a senior black congressman, Joshua Fairbanks, Noble was a member of a group Macon worked with mobilizing against investments in South Africa, demonstrating in front of the South African embassy against apartheid. Their arrest during a demonstration sealed their friendship.

A compact, whirling dervish of a man, Noble was prematurely gray and glided across a room like a panther. As the oldest son of one of Washington's most respected black preachers, Noble had inherited his father's eloquence and genius for rallying others to action. Often after long meetings plotting the defeat of apartheid, Noble asked Macon to join him for a drink or a late night snack. Noble Carson talked the way James Brown moved his feet. His conversation was incisive quick-witted poetry. He told her all the dirt about congressmen and senators on the Hill and viewed his job with a pragmatism that sometimes disheartened Macon.

One evening Macon met him in his office on the Hill. As they strolled down the halls of the Longworth Building, he said with a sweep of his arms, "Just look around, Macon, this is why blacks get elected and are never heard from again. This is Disneyland," he said, a wicked, raucous laugh echoing gently down the hall. "This is a place so comfortable, so nice, you never want to go home, and some of these guys never do." He told her about the Capitol gym, the bank, the medical services and the myriad perks that ensured congressional privilege and encouraged abuse of power. "What's a black politician gonna say when he gets stationed here except Thank you, boss?" he'd asked, squeezing her tight for emphasis and kissing her cheek playfully.

"Oh, Noble," she'd protested.

"Come on, Macon," he'd said as they left the building and headed for her car, "when was the last time you heard a member of the Black Caucus criticize Israel? Say anything about a subject that doesn't have to do with race? Rock the boat? Just like the white boys, they're bought and paid for. After a while you could do this blindfolded."

SHE LOVED TO listen to him talk, savored the sound of his laughter. She had been falling for him even then. Macon just hadn't known it.

NONETHELESS, SHE was really not surprised when he was arrested for stealing three hundred thousand dollars from the campaign chest of Joshua Fairbanks. She had heard rumors about his weakness for gambling. Macon had seen him in the eight-hundred-dollar suits he wore in the "glory days" as he

AND DO REMEMBER ME

called the period when he talked easily and casually with Senator Kennedy when he ran into him in the halls of the Rayburn Building. Those were the days when he twisted arms and made promises, all to raise money for Fairbanks. He had answered virtually to no one then, not even Fairbanks himself, so much was he trusted by his boss. The world, to Noble Carson, was an orchard and he entered it every day with an appetite and two skillful, fast-moving hands.

Sentenced to five years in prison, Noble served two and had been out on probation for the last year and a half. When Macon went to visit him at the federal penitentiary in Lewisburg, Pennsylvania, she asked him why he stole the money. As she sat waiting for his answer, she wondered if his was a political mistake or a personal tragedy?

"It was so easy," he told her. "So easy. It was there. I could do it. And I did. Lots of times the contributions came in the form of cash. Sometimes checks were made out to me, since I was the main fund-raiser. Josh trusted me. I cashed them."

Even in his prison uniform, Noble Carson looked suave, fashionable. Staring at him across the wooden picnic table in the visiting area, Macon thought that he looked better than she had seen him look in years. The haunted, hunted look of the weeks preceding his sentencing had given way to an unperturbed mellowness.

Yet beneath his calm exterior a furtive combustibility still lurked, a warm, radiant heat that Macon knew had fired both his political commitment and his greed. But it was this contradiction, this studied conflagration of cross purposes that defined Noble. Even sitting across from him in Lewisburg, Macon battled with the passion that shot across her heart like a meteor. Noble's arrogance and pride offended and seduced her. He would not admit to a moment of remorse; his only regret, he said, was that he had betrayed Fairbanks, who had been a mentor and friend. In the clubby, familial atmosphere of Capitol Hill, Fairbanks had relied so much on Noble's expertise and political skills that Fairbanks had vainly tried to cover up the theft. But a congressional committee got wind of the crime and forced Fairbanks to press charges.

When Noble revealed during Macon's visit that his wife Angela had filed for a divorce, Macon was surprised at the relief she felt. For, she had assured herself, no, she did not want Noble Carson. Never in a million years.

MACON ERASED THE messages on the answering machine and recalled that when she and Noble had gone out the previous week she had told him about the cancer, about how afraid she had been, how much she had wanted to live.

He told her about prison, saying, "There was a period, around the middle of my sentence, when being there was a relief. My creditors couldn't get to me. There were almost no decisions that I had to make for myself. I didn't have to try to impress anybody. Everybody there had fucked up. Nobody was pointing a finger."

"Are you saying you experienced a spiritual awakening in prison?" Macon asked.

"I wish I had," he said slowly. "I know this has been hard on our friendship, your view of me. You must think I let you down, that I sullied the reputation of the race, and affirmed everything white folks think about niggers with power." A brittle edge frosted his words.

"Noble, I don't give a damn what white folks think. But I was afraid for you."

"I don't want to tell you how many times I was afraid for me too."

"Are you seeing anyone?" he asked.

"Why do you want to know?"

"I have my reasons."

"Since the operation I've kind of avoided relationships."

"Oh, damn, Macon, I don't believe this, not you, in emotional retreat?"

"It takes time," she protested.

"I want to see you sometimes," he said, the request a soft kiss on her cheek. In response to her silence, he said, "Macon, I want to bring you flowers."

"Noble, I don't know," she said, wanting to run, wondering how he would feel if he saw her chest.

"I do," he insisted, his voice brisk with impatience, with the stubborn, take-charge force that she loved and hated at the same time.

"But we're friends. I don't want to lose that."

"How do you know we won't remain friends?"

"Lately, my track record hasn't been so great."

"Macon, I'm lonely. You don't have to say you are too. Just tell me I can take you out. That I can kiss you. Bring you flowers. Why can't you just say yes? I've been before one judge and jury. I don't need another one. Will you be my court of appeals?"

NOBLE HAD CALLED again, sounding happy to find her at home, and told Macon he would see her around eight-thirty. The house was a mess. Macon made a turkey sandwich and gobbled it down. She changed into jeans and a tee shirt and cleaned up the kitchen and the living room, deliberately, carefully, even vacuuming the floors and dusting the massive bookshelves. She cleaned the house in a frenzy of dedication and when she was done she fell on the sofa, her body moist with sweat, fatigue and exhilaration. But the desire was still there. She had not extinguished it as she had hoped. After a quick shower, she dried herself in front of the full-length mirror in her bedroom. Her doctor had proudly called the incision a clean cut. The skin where the cut was made had folded over into a soft flap. Macon stood before the mirror and caressed her breast and rubbed the skin over her chest. No man had seen her like this. For all the courage she liked to think she possessed, the thought of Noble seeing this terrified her. A week ago she had had a checkup—the blood test, the bone and liver scan—to see if the cancer had returned. The tests were all negative. But she would never again be able to take her life for granted.

WHEN NOBLE arrived, he kissed Macon gently, holding her close in the hallway before entering the living room. To her surprise, she did not resist him, but felt oddly relieved by the assertiveness of his touch.

She told him about the ransacking of the BSU offices, saying, "You know what frightens me most? Young people did this. Kids. I think I could handle it better if I knew adult Klansmen had done it. But if kids did this, what happens to the idea of each generation being an improvement over the one that preceded it? What am I doing in the classroom? What are any of us doing there?"

"Racism is a virus," Noble told her with a weary shake of his head. "And since nobody's really looking too hard for a cure it reproduces itself over and over again."

Noble was working as a consultant at a black think tank in downtown Washington, conducting research on shifts in black voting patterns in the last decade. He'd had a particularly rough day, he told her. "I'm not a desk man, somebody to sit in front of a computer and punch in statistics, graphs and all that. With Josh, I was his front man, the arm twister, the person who rallied the troops to reach into their pockets and pull out their checkbooks. I'm restless and bored doing research. And they know it."

Macon made Noble a rum and Coke and fixed herself a mug of herbal tea. They watched the late news. When Macon turned the television off, Noble told her, "You know my parole ends soon."

"If I didn't know better, I'd say you almost sound sad."

"In a way I am."

"You'll miss being on parole?"

"I'll miss my parole officer."

"You're kidding!" Macon exclaimed.

"No, I'm serious," Noble said, folding his hands behind his head, stretching his legs out before him. "He's a righteous dude. Righteous. Remember when we used to say that?" Noble winked at Macon. "He never made me feel like shit because I blew it. He just faced me man to man. Something my dad never did."

"Your father's a minister, what do you expect?"

"Yeah, it's been rough all these years mainly because he's never been my father, he's always been my minister," Noble said bitterly.

"And your parole officer?"

"I guess what I mean is—" Noble began.

"He forgave you."

"Yeah."

"The way your father hasn't."

"The way I'm scared he never will."

"You're his son. He knows that."

"Hell, I learned how to raise money, grease palms, how to soak the rich and the poor watching my daddy pastor a church." The words were vintage Noble-easy, enticing, only half true.

"Are you saying there's no difference between what you did for Fairbanks and what your father did in the name of God?"

"I wish I could, Macon. But even I'm not that bold," he admitted.

"Of course you are," Macon said.

"Can I be that bold tonight? Will you let me?" Noble asked softly, reaching across the length of the sofa, pulling her close to him. "I don't feel like being a gentleman," he whispered in her ear. "And, Macon, I don't want you to be a lady."

As soon as they walked into her bedroom, Macon turned off the lights, but Noble quickly turned on the lamp beside her bed. He unbuttoned her blouse, his fingers nimble and quick, as Macon stared at a corner of the room, afraid to look at his eyes when he saw her chest. He gently pushed the blouse over her shoulders and kissed her on her neck, whispering, "Relax, please, don't fight me, not now."

His plea was so deep, so real, that Macon gave in. She rested her arms on his shoulders as he unfastened her bra in the back. The prosthesis came off easily, and Noble laid it on the bed beside them. He kissed her there, kissed her there first, on the place where she had thought for so long that she was empty. Dead. Noble made tiny circles of kisses around the place where her breast had been and then gazed up at Macon and kissed her eyes, stalling the onslaught of tears. They lay in her bed for a long time Noble simply running his hands over her body, caressing her. When Macon reached for him, Noble said, "No, wait, let me make love to you."

Beneath his touch she was renewed, her body a continent he joyously discovered. Later, lying in his arms, Macon asked quietly, "Does it matter to you?"

"Not one bit," he said, letting his hand again rest there and gently fondle her. "One day it won't matter to you either," he assured her.

"Noble, I want to live," she sighed. "I want to live a long time."

"So do I, Macon, so do I."

THE LOW RESTLESS rumble of Edwin Braithwaite's snores woke Pearl from a fitful, unsatisfying sleep. Her leading man lay on his side, his body bunched like a fist. She was always surprised to wake up beside her lovers. Not once had she succeeded in erasing the memory of their touch, or the surprise of the morning after. But she kept trying.

Fatigued from a nearly sleepless night, she rolled on her back and stared at the ceiling. The play was in its last week in Washington; the run that had been extended earlier by two weeks. On tour for six months, Pearl wanted nothing more than to go back to New York. To go home. After Saturday night she would be free.

Pearl played the role of Wilhemena Grace. In the course of the play, her character aged from twenty to fifty-five. She was in virtually every scene, and she delivered a ten-minute monologue at the play's conclusion. Some nights after the play she could not sleep, her willful alter ego, much as she did in the play, refusing to release her grip on anyone who owed her allegiance, loyalty or love. But Wilhemena Grace had not haunted her sleep last night. Pearl had only dreamed about her father, as she had every night since his stroke.

"JESSIE, JESSIE, is that you?" Olive Foster had shouted into the phone, as though she were talking to her daughter across an ocean or a universe. Pearl had been in a hotel room in Philadelphia, three hours before an evening performance, when the call came.

"Yes, it's me, Mama." She knew her mother's voice. How could she forget it? She had spent most of her life wondering why this voice had not roused itself in her defense. She knew her mother's voice.

"Your daddy's took sick. Real sick," Olive blurted out quickly. "Had a stroke two days ago. He's in a coma. And it don't look good."

Pearl felt no relief, no sadness. She had no idea what to say. Mae Ann had kept Pearl informed of the hypertension, arthritis, then an attack of paralysis that virtually crippled Chester Foster in the last several years.

"You still there, Jessie?"

"Yes, ma'am, I'm here."

"Mae Ann was gonna call you, but I begged her to let me do it. I told her it was my place to tell you. You may not want me to be, but I am still your mama."

"What do the doctors say?" Jessie asked, as she nervously turned on the television and saw the taut, lean bodies of several basketball players fill the screen.

"Say we just have to wait and see if he comes out of the coma. He's been real sick a long time."

"Mae Ann told me."

"Was you mad at me too, Jessie? I know he hurt you. But you been mad at me all this time too? That why you never called or wrote, why you treat me like I'm less than a stranger?"

Pearl didn't say a word. She could barely breathe.

"Wasn't nothing I could do, Jessie."

"Mama, there's always something you can do. Something," she said, finding her voice.

"You gonna come home to see him?"

"Mama, I'm in the middle of a tour. I have a show to do every night. I can't just leave in the middle of a tour."

"Not less he dies. They'll let you come home then, won't they? You saying you can't come home till your father's dead. The man who gave you life."

"The man who raped me."

Her mother's startled sharp intake of breath whistled in Pearl's ear.

"He's dying, Jessie, he ain't got long. You got to forgive."

"Why do I have to forgive, Mama? Tell me why? He raped me."

It had taken years of sporadic, wrenching therapy for her to say the word. Pearl had hungered for the catharsis she had mastered on the stage to infiltrate her life. She went through four therapists to find one she thought she might be able to trust one day. The therapy sessions were worse, she concluded, than anything her father had done to her. Initially she approached the sessions as a drama in which she skillfully masked the truth, her powers of deception hard won and polished from years of practice. Only when the therapist threatened to end the sessions, to in effect "fire" her as a client, did Pearl begin to peel off the layers.

Knowledge carved her up. Healing hurt as much as being sick. If before she had wanted to die because of her childhood, now she longed for death because she understood too well the woman she had become. A new, fiery language took shape in her mind, took hold of her life and refused to let go.

Anger was intoxicating, it left her exhilarated, but in the end it offered no peace. But anger had introduced her to the proper names, the correct designations. Anger settled quite effectively some scores and she said again, "Mama, he raped me."

"Hush, girl, don't be saying that."

"What do you want me to call it, Mama? Give me a word to use instead."

"I shoulda knowd," Olive said wearily, "shoulda knowd you couldn't forgive. He's had his punishment. God made him pay."

Her mother was preaching again. Olive Foster was an assistant pastor at a storefront Evangelical church whose zealous young pastor had spotted Olive on a downtown street corner one afternoon, a Bible open to Timothy, her shrill, yearning voice halting passersby with its promise of redemption and eternal love. Reverend Cane Montgomery had marveled at the small crowd gathered around the stout, elderly woman whose vigorous pronouncements of the Word were rooted, he could tell, in a shame so deep it threatened to be everlasting.

But to Pearl, her mother's faith was a smoke screen, denying Olive Foster full entry into the region of her own specific pain.

"Did you ever wonder why I had to pay too, Mama?" Pearl asked, her voice breaking. "Why do you want to steal from me what I have a right to feel? I paid too. Mama, I've got to go now. Call me and tell me when I can come home. Call me and tell me when it'll finally be safe."

———

CHESTER FOSTER died at ten minutes after four, just as Pearl was walking on stage for a final curtain call during the Saturday matinee performance. The only witness to his death was his wife, who sat beside his bed as he silently slipped away. When he seemed no longer to be breathing, Olive Foster lifted her husband's wrist and felt for a pulse. She placed her ear against his chest and heard no heartbeat, then she gently closed his eyelids. She sat back down in the chair beside his bed and looked, for what she hoped would be the last time, at the tubes taped along Chester Foster's arms, the tubes running from his nose. His skin was withered, gray. The thick head of hair he had cherished as a younger man had begun falling out years before. Paralysis had deformed the muscles in his arms and hands so that his upper body resembled a twisted tree, split and shuddering with age. As Olive folded her hands in prayer, the only sound in the room was the hum of the television perched overhead. When she opened her eyes again, she gazed at her husband, thinking of the people she would now have to call, the plans she would have to make for the funeral. The first person she would call when she got home was Jessie.

THE PLAY HAD ended at ten-thirty and Pearl had fled immediately to her dressing room where she had locked the door and sat before the dressing table shivering with remorse and grief. She had chosen to go on, to perform, despite the call from her mother two hours before the curtain went up—the call that informed Pearl her father was dead.

Pearl usually used the period just before going on stage to rest, or to read something unrelated to the play. Sometimes she meditated. But no matter how she chose to use them, those hours were considered sacred.

The call lasted no more than five minutes. Her mother told her she could come home now, that the funeral would be Monday afternoon, that her father had died peacefully. Pearl promised she would come for the funeral, promised to leave Sunday night from Washington.

She had not once considered not going on, had told no one about the call. She was a professional and had performed her role without a hitch.

The party to celebrate the end of the tour was in full swing when she arrived at Macon's house.

"So they'll get off with a slap on the wrist, and a mandatory class in Race Relations 101," Pearl heard Macon say, as she neared the fireplace where Macon stood with Noble and Hilton Butler. Noble Carson's arm possessively circled Macon's waist, and he was nursing a drink in his other hand.

"I wouldn't call it a slap on the wrist," Hilton protested, shifting uncomfortably. "The group will have all activities suspended for the rest of the year. And why would you demean a course you recommended we create?"

"Hilton, they didn't just ransack an office. They destroyed the trust those students had in the university, its ability to speak for and protect them."

"I agree. How can I deny what you're saying? But there's only so much we can do. The president's office isn't a prosecutorial body and this order came straight from him."

"Macon thinks the university is special," Noble said, hugging her affectionately. "Like a black kid should have a greater chance of being struck by lightning than being called nigger on the average campus."

Macon spotted Pearl and pulled her close, disengaging herself from Noble's hold and hugging her friend. Then she introduced Pearl to Hilton. Noble, who'd met Pearl earlier, kissed her lightly on the cheek, saying, "You sure we can't get that play extended again?"

"I love D.C., the audiences are great. But, Noble, I'm ready to go home," Pearl sighed.

Several people surrounded Pearl, complimenting her on her performance. She stood in their midst, a smile on her face, her hands clammy and cold, and answered their questions as though walking through a dream. Behind her Noble and Macon were engaged in a vigorous, though friendly disagreement with Hilton. Pearl saw Edwin enter the room and he waved to her. She smiled at him, hoping he would rescue her.

Edwin expertly waded through the crowd and reached for Pearl's hand, apologizing as he claimed her.

"This is my leading lady, folks," he laughed gently. "We have to say our good-byes."

As they danced, Edwin told Pearl, "I'll miss you." Then he looked at her closer and said, "Damn, I know I'm good but those tears aren't for me are they?"

In response, Pearl buried her head in his chest. The hours spent in his bed or hers after making love, talking about the progress of their careers, cast members, best and worst experiences on the road, had meant so much. Edwin, whose fierce talent, keen features and tawny complexion had kept him modeling and then acting since he was eight, gave her advice as they lay wrapped in the sheets switching channels on the room's huge TV, ordering room service.

"You're an actor," he told her, "but don't think like one. Set up some kind of retirement plan." He told her how to invest her money the next time she got a windfall. "You won't always be young and pretty," he joked. "Act like that day is a month away instead of more years than you can imagine. Get some other kind of skill, anything so you'll be prepared for the day when black actresses who look and sound like you aren't in style anymore."

They had begun flirting in Chicago, had become lovers in Boston, had fought in Baltimore and had made up in Washington.

"I'll miss you too," she told him, thinking only of her father.

"I don't know what's wrong, Pearl, but whatever it is, it's not tougher than you are. You want me to take you back to the hotel?" He felt her trembling in his arms.

"No, Edwin, I'm okay. Really, I'm fine," she said, grateful the song was now over. Edwin hugged her one last time and when she turned to walk away from him she bumped into Macon.

For the first time that evening Macon looked closely at Pearl and she knew something was wrong. Reaching for Pearl's hand she led her upstairs to her bedroom. Closing the door, watching Pearl slump heavily onto the bed, Macon asked, "When did he die?"

Since Pearl had told her about her father's stroke, Macon had watched the changes in her, the tenseness, the anxiety. What had informed her so certainly of what had happened was the absence of all this in Pearl's demeanor. Sullen, sad resignation had replaced the anguish.

"Earlier today. I got the call from my mother before I went on."

"And the funeral?"

"It's Monday."

"You're going, aren't you?"

"Yes, I'm going. You know, after I hung up with her, I went to the mirror in the bathroom and I looked at my face and I saw how much I look like him. Macon, I look just like him."

"Pearl, I don't know what to say."

"You know, I always thought it was from him that I got my love of acting." This thought suddenly seemed too much for Pearl and she rose from the bed and walked over to the window. "When he was in a good mood at night, before we all went to bed, he'd sometimes tell us stories." An icy, bewildered smile suddenly appeared on her face. "Brer Rabbit and those kinds of stories. He'd be five, six different characters. He could change voices, expressions, everything. We all loved him so much then. When he was pretending to be somebody else." Pearl stopped. Then to Macon's amazement, she went on. "And he loved taking us to the movies with him and we'd sit up in the balcony in the dark. I think I got my drinking from him too," she said, her voice trailing off into a bitter whisper. "Most times he was drunk when he bothered me. When I got older, he'd make me drink with him, before it happened."

"Pearl, you don't have to go on, not if you don't want to," Macon cautioned.

"I told you what he did, but I never told you how it started," Pearl said, turning from the window to face Macon.

"The first time I was twelve and Mama was away. A relative nearby was sick and she'd gone to tend to them. I remember him coming in the room in the dark and waking me up. I remember his hands, his breath, his voice, as he hustled me out of bed. By that time he and Mama didn't sleep together much. He slept, most nights, on a small cot in the living room. When it started I just closed my eyes and pretended I was dreaming. I felt so small laying beside him. So small. And he said, 'Just touch it one time, Jessie,' he said. 'It won't hurt and it'll make Daddy feel real good. Since your mama ain't here.' I knew I shouldn't do it. I was scared what Mama would say and I put my hands under my back. He grabbed my hand and forced me to touch it. Like he was pulling my arm out of the socket. It felt wet and clammy and cold. And for some reason I thought at that moment about all the dead people I'd ever seen. Touching it made me feel the same way I felt when I looked at somebody dead. Then he put it between my legs and I could feel it inside me and nothing had ever hurt me so much. It's like I could feel it in every part of my body, and it's like it was pushing everything that was in me out of me. Nothing ever hurt me so bad. Not before or since. I tried to scream, but he covered my mouth with his hand."

Taking a deep breath, Pearl rushed on. "He made me wash up good afterward and told me not to tell anybody or he'd hurt me worse. He kept it up, even when Mama was there." She told Macon this, closing her eyes tightly, shaking her head as if she could not believe her own story. "The worse it got, the more Mama stayed out of his way, pretending not to know. And when I'd try to tell her, she wouldn't listen. That's when I started hating her, maybe even more than I hated him. And to this day, I don't know why I never got pregnant. The only explanation I can think of is that there is a God somewhere."

"Do you want me to go with you?" Macon asked, walking across the room, her arms open to Pearl.

"No, Macon. I have to do this alone."

REQUIEM

Sʜᴇ ᴛᴏʟᴅ ʜᴇʀsᴇʟғ she would not cry. Not for her father. Yet standing beside his casket, looking at his face—a placid, seamless mask in death—Pearl did cry. Love and hate had merged, reshaping memory with a finally perfect hand.

The house on Davis Road had been torn down long ago. Mae Ann's husband Tyrone had helped to purchase a new house for Chester and Olive Foster. But the new house, like the old one, was a haven for secrets. It was in the kitchen of this house that Chester Foster's children sat unearthing the past he had bequeathed. Their inheritance was as substantive as an illusion, as damning as a fingerprint.

In the years after Pearl left home, Chester Foster was one of the first blacks hired by the Columbus police force. Leaving his job as janitor behind, he studied for and gained his GED. He served on the force for nearly twenty years before his health was racked by repeated and serious illnesses. Once in uniform, he gained a reputation as the cop who could keep blacks in line.

Earlier that day the living room had been filled with police officers, stern-faced, officious, offering condolences to Olive Foster. The sight of the police officers entering the living room in a small but obtrusive phalanx, hushing conversation, made Pearl shiver. They've come years too late, she thought, years too late.

NOW THE HOUSE was quiet. The guests had left and Olive Foster had retreated to her room. Pearl sat across from her brother Willie, his bearded face a volatile map of competing emotions, his eyes fearsome shining sparks.

Pearl had told him, hugging him on Mae Ann's porch the day before he left for Viet Nam, "Come back, Willie, please come back."

He had returned, but with stubborn accusing voices lodged in his head, with flashbacks that transported him to hell in seconds. He had left a leg and a more substantial part of himself in some jungle he could no longer name.

In the end Willie had conquered the flashbacks, sealed himself against the voices and found steady work. It only took fifteen years. Pearl had clung to Willie all that day—at the cemetery, in the hearse, in their mother's house—holding onto him as he whispered stories about his visions in her ear, translated the curses the voices rained upon him, told her how he had found a way to heal. They had sat apart from the others on the front porch as Willie showed her the carvings he had begun to make once again. Sitting on the porch at dusk, Willie had held a beautifully carved eagle in his palms.

"For a long time when I came back," he told Pearl, "these

animals kept me from turning the knife on myself." A shop in Jackson had begun to sell his carvings and Willie was hoping to be able to devote more time to producing them.

Now, at the kitchen table, Willie told Pearl, "When I came back from Nam and told Daddy about the voices I was hearing, the funny thing was he understood. He was about the only one who didn't say I was crazy."

"What was he like at the end?" Pearl asked, longing but afraid to hear the answer, not daring even to look at Willie this time.

"He never said he was sorry," Willie laughed. "He changed but he was still the same. When that paralysis got to him real bad and he couldn't get around so good, or use his hands, he didn't have nothing to do but think, and I know he started seeing things different. It wasn't anything he said. But I could feel it in him. I'd come by the house, all crazy and feeling lost, sometimes not knowing what I was gonna do or was capable of doing the next second and I'd sit down and he'd tell me about the things he saw when he was in the Navy during World War II. He was a cook but he was close enough to war to get a smell of how awful it was."

"Did he ever talk about me?"

"All the time. One day, I'll never forget, we were watching television and we saw you doing a commercial for some kind of aspirin, or painkiller, and he near about fell off the sofa. He started calling Mama to come and see but by the time she came in the room you were gone from the screen. Couldn't nobody get a word out of him the rest of the day. He started watching TV from the moment it came on in the morning until it went off at night, just looking for a sight of you."

"I don't know why or how but I loved him," Pearl whispered.

"He was your daddy. He was your blood. Nothing you could do about it."

"Can you believe it? He's the only man I ever did love. And what he did kept me all these years from loving anybody else."

SHE HAD PROMISED not to cry, and swore never to forgive her mother. But when Willie and Mae Ann left, Pearl climbed the stairs to her mother's bedroom. She knocked on the door and heard her mother's voice inviting her in. Olive switched on the lamp beside her bed, and turned on her side to face Pearl. She patted a spot on the bed, inviting Pearl to sit beside her. A rotund, silver-haired woman quivering with energy, Olive Foster said gently, "Come here, Jessie, come here and tell me everything."

"Oh, Mama," Pearl whispered, "he's dead. And I don't feel one bit better."

Olive reached for her daughter, and held her as Pearl had not allowed her to do since her arrival that morning. Pearl had greeted her mother stiff with anger and grief, and the determination to hold Olive accountable blazed in her eyes. Now Olive felt her daughter's weary body grow pliable and suddenly surrender in her arms.

She would not talk to her this time about God. She would not ask her to forgive. For in the days since her husband's death, she had found herself unable to pray. Chester Foster was dead. And suddenly the idiom, the syntax of salvation, was erased from her tongue. She had to find her daughter. Then God would inspire her once again. But tonight she wouldn't put God between them, she'd reach out to Jessie with nothing but the truth.

The two women lay on the bed a long time—mother, daughter, stranger, enemy—the nearness of their bodies, their hunger for each other, articulating what they could never say.

But because they had been stripped so wrenchingly of speech, and by that of a means to find one another, Olive Foster broke the silence and said, as she stroked the thick braids of her daughter's corn-rowed hair, braids that reminded her of Jessie's hair at eight and ten sliding across her nimble fingers, "You done right well for yourself, Jessie. Right well. I'm proud of you."

"Thank you, ma'am."

"Tell me what it feel like when you be acting in front of all those people. How it make you feel?"

"I feel free, Mama. Like nothing bad ever happened to me. And nothing bad ever will. It's like the moment I'm in right then and there is the only moment that counts."

"You making a lot of money?"

"Sometimes I do. Sometimes I don't. But the money is like a bonus. I'd do it, I'd act for free, if I had to."

"How come you never got married, Jess?"

"How could I, Mama?"

"Wasn't there nobody ever loved you? Ever wanted to marry you?"

"One time there was."

"And children, Jess, you ever want children?"

"Mama, I never did. Never. I fixed it so I can't have any."

"I guess you must hate me."

"There's been times I did, Mama. But hate wore me out, beat me down so much I had to let it go. . . . Mama, how come you never made him stop? How come you never said nothing?"

"Jessie, you don't know. You just don't know. You an actress so you think words come easy, think they's always there for you. But between a man and a woman, a husband and a wife, sometimes words is the first thing to go, the first thing they lose. And feelings is all they got left. And because there's no words for the feelings, the feelings turn on you, get all messed up, locked up, stored up inside. And when they come out they come out the wrong way."

Pearl felt her mother's hand heavy and tense on her shoulder, heard her anguished breathing.

"How could I ask him to stop doing something I didn't even want to think about? Jessie, you just don't know. You just don't know."

Olive released Pearl and moved to her bureau where she brought out a cotton nightgown. In front of her daughter she removed her clothes and slipped into the gown and a robe. Then she sat down in a rocking chair near the window, and told Pearl, "When I met your daddy, I'd been preaching around at some of the little churches in Columbus for about three or four years. Preaching, can you imagine that? Nobody had never seen nothing like it, a little girl in the pulpit. But I got called, directly by God, when I was thirteen. I spoke in tongues, and do you know I even healed folks, healed folks with these hands." Olive held her tiny hands before her as though presenting Pearl with conclusive evidence of a miracle. "These hands. All the churches around Columbus would be filled when I'd be preaching, preaching from instinct, from something that had been planted deep inside me long before I studied the Word. My folks didn't have nothing really, they was just like all the other folks in the Delta and they was hoping my preaching would give em something. I hoped so too. Even the ministers that thought because I was a little girl it had to be Satan speaking through me and not God would ask me to preach at their churches cause I could fill em up. And I started to making a little extra money from all that preaching and was able to help my family some. By the time I was fifteen or so, I knew a normal woman's life wasn't for me. The feeling you say you get when you be acting, well that's the feeling I got preaching, like it wasn't nobody there in the room but me and God. And I was glad to be His instrument.

"But when I got a good bit older I wanted to be a normal woman too. God's hand began to feel real heavy on me, Jess, real heavy. I was preaching bout love thy neighbor and I'd look out on the congregation and covet the men staring up at me. Got to a point, Jess, where God wasn't enough. Wasn't nobody I could tell this to, cause I had been chosen, I was special. And I knew to go against my calling would be a sin.

"Then I met your daddy. He stayed with us the summer of '47. From the moment I saw him, it was a battle between him and God for me. All the feelings I'd been having, the longings, come to rest on him. But maybe that's why I wanted him. Everything that had come out of my mouth, everything I'd done, everything I'd thought, had to be good in the eyes of the Lord. But then why did the Lord give me the feelings your daddy stirred up in me? Why, Jessie, why?" Olive asked, her face a tangle of confusion beneath the room's mute shadows, her voice clear and thin.

Clutching the collar of her robe, Olive said, "My mama and daddy was always threatening that summer to throw my brother Lonnie and your daddy out the house for coming in all hours, gambling, running after women. But they'd give Mama and Daddy a few dollars to help with the food and that would buy em off. I couldn't get enough of just looking at your daddy. The more I prayed to resist him, the more I felt myself sinking. Then it seemed like he got tired of chasing whores and wanted something else. It was my duty to witness to him, to try and save his soul.

"One day when we was in the house by ourselves, I just walked up to him, and sat down beside him with the Bible in my hand, and told him, 'Chester Foster, the Lord wants your soul.' He smiled at me, that gold tooth of his shining, and he says, 'Miss Reverend Olive, if you here on the Lord's behalf, you can have my soul and anything else you want.'

"Pretty soon, near about everything I said to Chester Foster or did with him, I had to try to hide from my folks and ask the Lord to forgive. I was confused, Jessie, so confused cause all the feelings your daddy was stirring up in me was real feelings. They didn't feel bad, not all the time, like I'd thought they would. Then, when I got pregnant, we got married. He wasn't headed nowhere, except the next crap game, but it surprised me how he married me, without a thought, didn't even try to get out of it, like I thought he would. But he still run after the women and the good times.

"Wasn't no pulpit I could stand in now. And so I give it up, just give it up, my gift and its promise. He wasn't always mean, Jess, not all the time. There was times when there wasn't no women in his life cept me, from what I could tell. There'd be times he was a good husband. But then it would start all over again. Me never being enough for him. Him having to have other women too."

"But why did he start bothering me, Mama, why?"

"You want me to give you an answer that'll make all the pain you've suffered go away. I can't give you that, Jess. I was afraid, and small and sick. I had these tumors growing inside me and I was bleeding all the time. When they took out the tumors, Jess, I didn't feel nothin no more. Not a thing. I was tired and I was hurting all over. I felt bad, but I never could feel good. When your daddy touched me, I'd feel pain. When my body couldn't feel good it's like my mind couldn't neither. Then he started with other women again. I think, Jess, you was just another woman to him. Just another woman. When he was doing those things to you, you was just another woman."

"No, Mama, I was me. And I was his daughter."

"You want to hate me because I was weak, because I didn't stand up for you? Jess, I never stood up for myself. And after you left, I was gonna leave too. Seeing you run like that broke my heart, but give me courage. I was gonna leave. But when I told him, he got that old rifle he kept around the house and said if I did, if I left with his children, he'd kill hisself, stood in front of me with the rifle cocked, pointing at his stomach, and said he'd do it. So I stayed. Then when Mae Ann and Willie and Junior left home I was so used to staying I couldn't think of leaving. He was sick by that time and he couldn't hurt me no more than he already had."

"Mae Ann told me he said he'd kill me if I came back," Pearl said, nearly choking at the memory of the threat.

"Jessie, after you left, he was always walking around the house threatening to kill hisself, did she tell you that? He was scared you was gonna tell what he did. Scared folks would know.

"And all the time you locked me out too, Mama, why? Why me too?"

"I didn't know what to say. Every time I looked at you I saw how I was letting you down. After a while, it was easier not to look at you at all. All those years I lost you, Jessie. Losing you was the worst."

That night Pearl slept beside her mother. And in the middle of the night she woke up, woke in the midst of sleep the way she used to. She shivered beneath the cool breeze coming in through the window and moved closer to her mother. There was nowhere else to go. Pearl snuggled against her. She lay, her mother's echo, her linear frame.

There would be no more sleep tonight. She was still lost. But she had found her way home. Her mother had said, "Jessie, tell me everything," but where would she begin? Once she started, where would she stop? Mothers are daughters, their yearnings transposed, voices seeking perfect pitch. What would she say? she wondered. Dare she tell what living had required her to forget? Mothers are daughters choosing the end of their own story, guiding others to sculpt their own. Mothers are daughters too. Her mother's bitter song still rang in her ears. Until dawn arrived, she would be obsessed with her mother's plea, "Jessie tell me everything." In the morning, she would try.

About the Author

MARITA GOLDEN is the author of *Migrations of the Heart*, *A Woman's Place*, and *Long Distance Life*. Her writing has appeared in the *New York Times*, the *Washington Post*, and numerous other publications. She teaches in an M.F.A. program at George Mason University and lives with her husband and son in Washington, D.C.

Printed in the United States
by Baker & Taylor Publisher Services